W9-BAO-176

Guthrie couldn't speak.

Reaching over, he pulled Hannah to him.
He just wanted to comfort her. But the feeling
of her softness in his arms went to his head.
He kissed her hair, fragrant of spices, then
her eyebrows. Her eyes closed. He kissed
her eyelids, first one, then the other. Petal
soft. Such softness brought feelings, emotions
bubbling up from deep inside him.

Tilting up her chin, Hannah smoothed back his
golden hair, then rested her hand on his chest.

A warmth, healing and vital, flowed through
him like a cleansing prayer. "Hannah, you're
a wonderful woman. You make me believe…"
Maybe *he* might get a second chance, after all.

Books by Lyn Cote

Love Inspired

Never Alone #30
New Man in Town #66
Hope's Garden #111
Finally Home #137

LYN COTE

Born in Texas, raised in Illinois on the shore of Lake Michigan, Lyn now lives in Iowa with her real-life hero and their son and daughter—both teens. Lyn has spent her adult life as a teacher, then a full-time mom, now a writer.

When she married her hero over twenty years ago, she "married" the north woods of Wisconsin, too. Recently she and her husband bought a fixer-upper cabin on a lake there. Lyn spends most of each summer sitting by the lake, writing. As she writes, her Siamese cat, Shadow, likes to curl up on Lyn's lap to keep her company. By the way, Lyn's last name is pronounced "Coty."

Finally Home
Lyn Cote

Love Inspired®

Published by Steeple Hill Books™

STEEPLE HILL BOOKS

ISBN 0-373-87144-9

FINALLY HOME

Copyright © 2001 by Lyn Cote

This edition published by arrangement with Steeple Hill Books.

® and TM are trademarks of Steeple Hill Books, used under license. Trademarks indicated with ® are registered in the United States Patent and Trademark Office, the Canadian Trade Marks Office and in other countries.

Visit us at www.steeplehill.com

Printed in U.S.A.

Forgive us our trespasses
as we forgive those who trespass against us.
—The Lord's Prayer

With love to my sweet sister, Carole;
with thanks to Pat Birkett-Roby, my friend
and the Prairie Cook, who inspired Hannah's career.
And thanks to Cousin Jane,
who remembered party games I'd forgotten!

Prologue

~~

"That can't be our sister!" Doree shut her large blue eyes, then opened them again.

Spring turned gracefully in her seat at the restaurant table to view the woman who'd just entered. "Oh, my, what has Hannah done?"

"Thank you for that characteristic understatement." Doree continued to gawk. "Aliens must have sent an impostor in Hannah's place. She's wearing lime green!"

"Designer lime green," Spring added.

"You would notice that."

"*Anyone* could see that," Spring answered without offense.

Hannah Kirkland strode toward the table across a thick teal carpet. Both her sisters looked just as she had pictured them. Spring in a blue linen suit of impeccable cut. And in spite of the first-class restaurant setting, Doree in jeans and a UW Madison red-and-white Badger T-shirt. With a confidence she didn't feel, Hannah sat down, straightened the hem on the short skirt of her new linen suit, then checked the neckline of its ivory silk blouse. She tossed her head, letting her fifty-dollar haircut swing, then settle into its new, sophisticated style.

Only then did she speak. "Doree, I heard every word you said. When are you going to learn to lower your voice? Now close your lips. You look like a largemouth bass."

"Well," the redoubtable Doree replied, "do you know what you look like?"

Spring touched Doree's arm. "Hannah looks like an attractive young woman, just as she always has."

Grateful to Spring for her kindness, Hannah blinked back tears. She'd known exactly how both her sisters would react. No surprises. Spring, tactful. Doree, outspoken. But something in Spring's gaze caught Hannah's eye. Was Spring worried?

"How are you, dear?" Spring asked in her soft, caring voice.

"I am better than I was." Hannah lifted her chin.

Both Spring and Doree stared at her.

"What does that mean?" Doree asked. "What gives, dear sweet Honey? I thought you'd still be wearing your sensible bun and dove gray suit or maybe black for mourning dear Edward."

"Stop right now." Spring glared at Doree.

Hannah sighed. "It's all right, Spring. Our little sister is just being her brash self." She'd taken great pains with her appearance today, and her haircut, makeup and trendy clothing rivaled Spring's ever polished style. It all made Hannah feel as though she were masquerading as someone else. But after breaking up with her fiancé this spring, she had needed to take some positive action or give in to despair. Something she wouldn't do!

"Doree was raised to be polite and kind," Spring said sternly.

Hannah sat more comfortably in her seat, trying to relax. At the end after months of doubt, breaking the engagement had almost been a relief. More and more, she'd discovered Edward wasn't the caring man she'd imagined him to be. In fact, she'd begun to suspect she'd created her own perception of him, which had nothing to do with the opinionated man she'd discovered under her nose. "It's all right. I've been through a lot in the last few months, but the pain was less than I thought it would be. Really."

Spring nodded, then pushed her long golden hair over her shoulder. With arms folded skeptically, Doree watched them both.

Hannah noted an edge to Spring's voice. She'd have to get a private word with her, but now she decided was the time to implement another change. "One thing, though, I'd really like to leave my nickname, Honey, behind me. Would you please call me Hannah from now on?"

Doree and Spring exchanged startled glances. The waiter came to take their drink order, then left them.

Before Doree could put in any more provocative remarks, Hannah spoke up. "Lunch is on me today."

She opened the large gold-embossed menu. "I'm ordering lobster." From behind the tall impressive menu, she couldn't see, but she sensed her sisters' surprise.

"Works for me." Doree put her unopened menu on the array of silver and china. "Make that two. A poor college student like me has a hard time remembering what any shellfish tastes like, much less lobster. I can taste the drawn butter already. Yum."

A moment passed while Spring perused the menu. Hannah let the soothing atmosphere of the luxurious restaurant—the murmur of voices, the clink of ice and the occasional chuckle—work on her, relax her. The waiter returned with their iced teas.

Hannah smiled at him. "Two lobster luncheons with baked potatoes. Double butter and sour cream for my younger sister. Spring?"

Spring closed her menu. "The Caesar salad please."

"Large?" The waiter held his pen poised.

"No, small."

The waiter accepted the three menus and hurried away.

Hannah was splurging by ordering the lobster. She'd always been the one who had to watch her waistline. Spring seemed able to exist on air, while Doree's metabolism burned calories like a blast furnace.

"Sheesh!" Doree groaned. "Are you ever going to develop an appetite?"

"Probably before you develop adult manners," Spring replied without heat.

Doree leaned forward to continue the tiff.

Hannah held up her hand like a referee. "I invited you here to discuss Mom and Dad, not my wardrobe or Spring's appetite. That's the agenda. Stick to it, Doree, or you'll be paying your own check."

Doree wrinkled her tanned nose. Her short blond hair had been nearly bleached white by the summer sun. "Take it easy. I'll be good. It's just so much fun to get a rise out of you two."

Hannah ignored Doree's flippant comment. Doree had a good heart. With her first year of college under her belt, she'd spent the summer working with children in the Head-Start program here in Milwaukee. But as the baby of the family, Doree wanted it both ways. She insisted she be taken seriously while at times still acting as the family rebel and tease.

Spring fidgeted with the gold chain around her neck. This uncharacteristic sign of nervousness in Spring held Hannah's attention. Hannah discreetly eyed her older sister. Spring, in charge of community relations at Milwaukee's renowned Botanical Gardens, never seemed ill at ease, but she definitely was today.

After taking a deep breath, Spring returned Hannah's gaze, then asked, "Do you know something about Mother and Father we don't?"

This question startled Hannah. "No, their plans and medical conditions are about the same."

"I was afraid you had bad news for us," Doree

mumbled in a subdued tone. "I thought Mom's leukemia had started up again." She lowered her gaze to the white linen tablecloth.

Hannah's stomach tightened with guilt. "I'm sorry I worried you," she murmured with real regret. Was this what was concerning Spring?

Spring took a sip of iced tea, then held her glass in front of her mouth as though concealing her expression. "I was worried, too, but I've also been worried about their making this move to Petite Portage, especially now that Dad's heart is giving him trouble."

Hannah nodded. "I have, too."

Doree sat back and challenged them both with a tart smile. "Why? I think this is just what Mom needs. The pressure of being the perfect pastor's wife of a large congregation—"

"Father has been under the same pressure." Spring set her glass down.

"Both of them needed a change." Like setting lids on two simmering pots, Hannah extended a hand palm-down toward each sister. This had always been her role, the middle child, the peacemaker. "But change can be very difficult on people nearing retirement."

"I read an article about that in an applied psych class." Doree nodded with a serious expression. "Moving can really stress people."

"Exactly. So I've decided to go to Petite Portage and help them get settled." Hannah observed her sisters for their reactions.

"Can you get away?" Spring nervously rearranged the salt and pepper shakers, not making eye contact.

Hannah studied Spring. Her beautiful and intelligent sister always kept her own counsel. What else was she keeping under wraps today? "Yes, I can fax in my column from anywhere. And I've already talked to someone who wants to sublet my apartment for the remainder of this year. I called Mom this week. She and Dad are leaving tomorrow. They are going on a few side trips, then they plan to move into a room with a kitchenette at a local motel for a few weeks until their house is done."

"What about your food styling shoots?" Glancing up, Spring asked another practical question. "Don't you have several food photos to do for that special corn oil promotion?"

"I'm going to arrange a few field shoots in Petite Portage, letting the corn oil company advertising team make use of some local color. I thought I could use Mom's new kitchen. Maybe visit a cornfield—"

"Yeah, a little town in central Wisconsin will really jazz things up." Doree smirked.

Fingering her neck chain again, Spring ignored Doree. "When will the new house be done?"

"Their contract specifies three weeks from now, August thirty-first, but Dad mentioned something about delays—"

"Uh-oh." Doree sounded the alarm.

"Exactly." Hannah leaned her elbows on the table. "Someone needs to make certain our good-natured parents don't get taken advantage of."

Looking more concerned, Spring nodded. "I didn't agree with their signing with such a small builder—"

"That's because you didn't meet Guthrie Thomas!" Doree's face crinkled with amusement. "What a hunk! Blond. Muscles. Wow. He could build something for me any day of the week!"

Both Hannah and Spring frowned at Doree, who chuckled, then shrugged.

"Where will you stay?" Spring probed.

"I asked Dad to reserve me a room at the local motel also," Hannah replied.

"Thank you, Hannah." Spring smiled, and her face relaxed momentarily. "I appreciate your doing this. But if you need help, just call. I'll come right out."

The conversation paused while the waiter brought a basket of hard rolls and filled their glasses. He smiled and proceeded to the next table.

Spring caught Doree's eye, then Hannah's, then glanced down. "I hate to bring up another serious concern, but I think this is the time to discuss it."

Hannah braced herself for more bad news. Now they'd find out what caused Spring's fidgeting.

Still hesitating, Spring rearranged the butter dish and sugar bowl. "With Doree leaving to go back to school in Madison and your going to be with Mother and Father, we may not be together again until Thanksgiving or even Christmas."

"What is it?" Doree picked up a crusty roll and tore it in two.

Spring continued in her soft voice, "Last June after Mother was diagnosed with leukemia, I started reading as much as I could about the disease. I wanted to be able to understand what was happening.''

Hannah nodded, encouraging Spring.

"So?'' Doree prompted.

Spring sighed. "You remember how the doctor had the three of us tested as possible donors, in case Mother needed a bone marrow transplant?''

"Yeah?'' Doree slathered half her roll with butter.

"Didn't it bother you that we were Mother's only known blood relatives?'' Finally, Spring made eye contact with both of them.

Doree paused. She dumped the roll on the plate. "Yes, it did.''

Hannah nodded. "None of us matched.'' The pain of that memory squeezed inside her, making her catch a breath. She recognized the same deep distress on the stricken faces of her two sisters. Their mother had needed them, and they'd been helpless!

"What are you driving at?'' Doree asked. "Do you think we should try to find Mom's natural parents?''

"So I'm not the only one who thought of starting a search?'' Spring asked sounding relieved.

Doree pursued it. "But wouldn't Mom's natural parents be dead by now? I mean, Mom was born in 1945.''

Spring shook her head. "That means Mom's only in her fifties. Her adoptive parents both died early, before they even retired. But her natural parents would probably be in their seventies, and they could still be alive and active.''

"But Mother had always refused to look into her

past, her adoption,'' Hannah objected. "She said she'd never wanted to be disloyal to her adoptive parents!'' The idea of going against her mother's wishes startled her most. "She was even upset with the doctor when he suggested she should search for blood relatives.''

"I realize that, but I think Mother's leukemia makes the difference. What if this period of remission ends a few years from now and what if her leukemia progresses to the point where we need a match? What do we do then?'' Spring's gaze lingered on Hannah.

Her elbow on the table, Doree rested her chin on the back of her hand and considered Spring. "You mean, Spring, the perfect daughter, that we should go against our mother's wishes?''

"That is exactly what I mean.'' Spring pulled her shoulders back, sitting up straighter.

"As I live and breathe.'' Doree shook her head as if she couldn't believe her ears.

Hannah waved an impatient hand toward her younger sister. This wasn't time for teasing. "You mean without telling Mom or even Dad?''

Spring moved forward in her chair. "Yes. If you are there while they're moving in—''

"Right!'' Doree grinned. "You could look for Mom's adoption papers. See if any names or places were listed.''

Hannah frowned. She understood Spring's reasoning, but doing what she asked went against everything they'd been taught by their parents. She gazed at

Spring and recognized the same worry and doubt in her eyes. "I don't like going behind Mom's back."

"I wouldn't suggest it, either, under normal circumstances." Spring's voice had thickened with emotion.

"But it's for Mom's good and Dad's," Doree said. "They've been married thirty-five years. Moving is stressful, but not as much as losing a life partner!"

Wishing Doree hadn't voiced those awful words, Hannah stared at her hands. "I will have to take some time to think and pray about this."

Doree piped up. "Hey, I've already started—"

"We'll all pray about it." Spring warned Doree with a pointed look. "But it will be your decision, Hannah. I wouldn't ask you to do something you thought was wrong."

Hannah nodded. She knew Spring was being kind, but the reality of the situation was that she alone would carry the burden of this decision, one that might violate her conscience and could mean life or death to their mother.

Chapter One

~≈~

Two weeks later, with Dad's hand-drawn map on the seat beside her, Hannah glanced ahead and made a right turn at Humphreys Road. Her parents' future home should be about three-fourths of a mile ahead on the right. After another week of cloudy weather and heavy rain, today had dawned bright and warm.

On her way to Petite Portage, she'd chosen to take the back roads through kelly-green cornfields and sage-green cabbage fields. She'd stopped for lunch at a small hometown restaurant. There, in a lively conversation with the cook, she'd picked up two new recipes, one for preparing wild pheasant and one for wild duck. They'd make great topics in her fall columns.

Now on her way down Humphreys Road, Hannah passed three widely spaced houses, two newer ranch styles and one old farmhouse, then came to a dead end. She stopped, studied the map again, turned around. This time she drove like a snail, keeping her eyes to the left side of road. She found it, a muddy gravel track without a house in progress in sight. She turned in. At its end, she stopped.

Oh, no. Her mind repeated this phrase several times. With a sinking heart, she put her car in ''park'' and got out. Crows squawked overhead. Beneath her feet, soft ground under grass, then ahead, mud with a path of boards spanning it. A field of mud with truck-tire tracks carved through it in a deep criss-cross pattern, stray hillocks of muddy grass, stacks of lumber under heavy blue plastic tarps. A concrete foundation.

No house.

Just a foundation.

''I'm dreaming this,'' she whispered in the quiet of the country. ''This house is supposed to be complete in eight days.''

Things like this take time. Edward's irritating voice echoed in her memory and set her teeth on edge. How many times had she endured hearing Edward say that galling phrase? Over the past three years, she'd put up with too much too long. Never again.

She could imagine all the builder's polite excuses. *Bad weather slowed construction. Building materials shortage. Had trouble getting quality workmen.* Each phrase turned up the heat higher under her simmering temper. ''Guthrie Thomas,'' she growled to the place where her parents' house should have been. ''I am not buying any excuses. My parents paid good money and signed a contract in good faith with you. If you couldn't fulfill the contract, you should have released them and let someone else build it.''

Edward's disembodied voice interrupted. *But, Honey, things can't always run on your schedule.*

"Shut up, Edward!" Hannah declared. "And don't call me Honey! I'm not sweet, little Honey Kirkland anymore!"

She charged back to her fire-engine-red sport utility vehicle, got in and slammed the door. She started the car, then threw it into reverse. Mud flew up around her tires. At the road's edge, she ground to a halt, cast a hasty glance each way, then shot onto the deserted road. She shoved the gearshift back into "drive" and took off with squealing tires.

The powerful motor under the hood charged her with adrenaline, momentum. Consigned to the unappetizing past, she'd left Edward and her VW bug behind in Milwaukee. The last fourteen months had been the most difficult of her twenty-five years. A broken engagement, then.... "I was a fool, a blind little wimp," she muttered.

With only a sustained pause, she slid by the stop sign at the empty crossroads, then barreled down the two-lane highway into town. She blew past the "Reduced Speed Ahead" sign and didn't slow until she saw the city limits sign, "Petite Portage—Population 2356—Speed Limit 25 M.P.H."

Still pushing the speed limit, she swept through town looking for the small motel where her parents were staying. Within minutes, she slowed on Front Street. Ahead, a red-and-white painted sign announced Hanson's Cozy Motel with a green neon Yes over Vacancy. The motel, a one-story white building with six red doors in a row, also had an attached restaurant, Hanson's Cozy Café.

Hannah had found her parents' temporary home. She rolled to a stop in front of the motel office. She'd barely stopped and exited her vehicle before a large woman in blue polyester stretch pants and a hot pink T-shirt that proclaimed her to be the World's Best Grandma hurried out of the office.

"You must be the Kirkland girl! I'm Mrs. Fink, Lila Fink, the owner. Welcome to Petite! You're just going to love it here! Your parents are great people. I knew it the moment I laid eyes on them!"

The flow of words sloshed over Hannah. She floundered in the sensation of being swept up in a rushing current. She said the first words that came to mind. "But this is Hanson's Cozy Motel."

The large woman shook with laughter. "Sure it is! Would anyone stay at Fink's Cozy Motel?"

Hannah could think of no reply to this, but Lila efficiently produced a plastic-tagged key, then led her to a small room. Hannah assessed the room, and her mood slipped another notch. Obviously Mrs. Fink had decorated the Cozy Motel thirty years ago. Avocado green and gold vinyl reigned supreme. But the off-white paint on the walls gleamed, and the brown shag carpet had been steam-cleaned recently.

Lila pressed a key with a bronze plastic tag printed with a large two into Hannah's hand. "I'll let you get settled. Then we can get to know each other."

"My parents?" Hannah prompted.

"They can't wait to see you. They told me, 'Honey is coming today.'"

"Where are they?" Hannah asked, trying to hold her own against the flow of words.

"They're at the church. They spend most of their days there. I only get to talk to them in the café in the mornings—"

"Where's the church?" Hannah edged toward the door.

"It's easy to find. Everything in Petite is easy to find." Lila chuckled. "Just go back up Front Street and turn right, go about half a mile, you can't miss it. I walk there on nice Sunday mornings—"

Escaping, Hannah smiled, waved and jumped into her car. Back up Front Street, she drove half a block then turned right. She wasn't surprised that her parents spent their days at the church. Good grief! Mrs. Fink rattled on more than Edward's mother, and that woman could talk the hind leg off a horse!

"This isn't happening," Hannah told the steering wheel. She pressed down on the gas pedal.

Instantly, a police siren 'burped' just behind her. A look in her rearview mirror confirmed a police car nearly touched her rear bumper. "Where did he come from? Thin air?" She pulled over.

A tall, lanky police officer who didn't look old enough to shave appeared at her window. "Hi, do you need any help?"

Of all the words she might have imagined this junior office asking, these weren't them. "What?"

He pointed back to where she had turned. "You were driving kind of fast and I didn't recognize your car. I thought you might need help, directions or something." He gazed at her, hope in his eyes.

"Aren't you a little young to be a police officer?" She asked feeling like Alice after she'd passed through the looking glass.

"I'm eighteen and I'm going to go to college this fall in law enforcement. But my dad had to testify in court at the county seat today, so he deputized me to keep an eye on things. It's been pretty boring. Are you sure you don't need—"

"I'm just driving down to the church."

He hung his head like a scolded puppy. "Okay."

"May I leave?"

"Sure. Just wanted to help." Mournful, he took a step back.

She moved the gearshift into drive and headed on. "Good grief!" She had the sensation that she'd driven a bit too far that day. Around the bend maybe?

The white steeple loomed ahead. As she pulled into the small parking lot, she gathered the scattered pieces of her purpose for coming to the church. Mrs. Fink and Officer Peach-fuzz had thrown her a bit off stride, but she wouldn't take excuses. She'd find out from her parents where the builder was and she'd have a talk with him today regardless of what her parents might say. The house should be nearly built by now, not barely begun.

If the builder couldn't deliver on time, she'd do everything she could to persuade her parents to enforce the contract deadline, no excuses. She wasn't going to let any man give her the runaround, as Edward had, ever again.

When she parked and slipped out of the car, the sound of hammer on wood greeted her. Well, something was getting built in Petite today!

Hannah recognized her parents' ten-year-old blue sedan parked beside the quaint one-story classic white prairie chapel. Good. They were here, as reported by Mrs. Fink. Hannah edged around the grassy side of the church, following the noise of the hammering. The squishy, soaked grass underfoot wet her shoes. She tried to ignore it.

Looking skyward, she noted the church's roof had been stripped of shingles. One patch of new plywood looked out of place above the period building, but the majority of the roof looked old and discolored with water damage. What was going on?

She halted, stunned by the man she saw straddling the peak of the roof facing the steeple.

Definitely the most perfect male she'd ever seen in real life. He wore no shirt. Tanned brown, his chest, shoulders and arms bulged with muscles. Real muscles, not the kind a man got from working out at a gym. His firm legs stretched against the tight blue denim covering them. Heaven in blue jeans.

She watched him lift the billed cap off his head and swipe his forehead with his arm, obviously brushing away the sweat on his brow. Sunlight glinted on golden waves.

Hannah swallowed with difficulty.

The man settled the hat on his head and eased up. Cautiously he balanced himself until he squatted, perfectly poised. Was he going into the steeple?

Feeling her pulse racing, Hannah wished he'd get down from the roof. He was making her nervous. Shouldn't he be wearing a safety harness or something?

A flicker of movement caught her eye. She followed the man's gaze and saw, in the opening at the bottom of the steeple, her father reaching out.

"No! Daddy, don't!" Her shout echoed in the stillness.

The man on the peak lost his balance. He tried to catch himself on a roofing rack. He couldn't.

Hannah shrieked.

Chapter Two

Horrified, she watched the man sliding down the side of the bare roof on his rump. He hit the gutter. It launched him forward.

Hannah screamed and closed her eyes.

He landed with a sickening thud facedown in the nearby grass.

She rushed to his side and knelt. With shaking fingers, she took his wrist to check for a pulse. His heart was still beating, racing, in fact.

"Oh!" Her mother ran toward her. "Is he all right?"

"He's got a pulse." *Thank you, God!*

"Is he breathing?" her father shouted as he came around a corner of the church.

Hannah rested her hand on the man's broad back. No. He wasn't taking breaths. "Call nine one one!"

The strong back under her hand shuddered. The man rolled over. He spit out a wad of grass and sputtered, trying to rid himself of green grass particles in his mouth. Grass clippings stuck to his face and hair. His eyes opened. Grass matted his thick eyelashes.

"Oh, Guthrie!" her mother exclaimed. "You're alive!"

Forcing down her budding hysteria, Hannah turned to her mother and caught her hands. "Sit down and lower your head. You're as white as a sheet!"

Mom obeyed, but she gasped, "You look as white as a ghost yourself. You sit down, too."

Concerned, Hannah turned to her father, who stood about ten feet away trying to catch his breath. "Dad?"

He held up a hand. "Okay... I'm okay. Take care of Guthrie."

Hannah went to her original victim. She'd arrived in Petite and in less than an hour nearly finished off her parents and their builder! This man fit Doree's description to a T. Guthrie Thomas, the hunk, the very man she had intended to tell off!

She knelt by Guthrie again. "You landed in a pile of grass clippings. Do you hurt anywhere?"

He sat up. With his knees bent, his elbows propped on them and his head bowed, he drew in deep breaths. "I just fell off a roof, lady."

"I know. I screamed."

"I heard you."

The vision of him catapulting toward her flashed in her mind. "Why weren't you wearing a safety belt?" she accused.

"Because I wasn't driving a car!" he gasped. "I

wasn't going to do any more work. I was taking another look at the steeple from outside." Stiffly, he pulled out a faded blue bandanna from his pocket, wiped his face and noisily blew his nose. "I've got grass all the way up my nose." He looked into her eyes. "Why did you scream?"

Weakness snaked through her. "I thought my dad was going to get out on the roof."

"I'd never let him do that. He just wanted to give me a hand in."

Hannah sat down and lowered her head.

"Feeling faint?" Guthrie asked.

Embarrassed by the first impression she'd made, she nodded. "I'm so sorry, Mr. Thomas."

"Me, too." Guthrie gave her a lopsided grin.

In the cooler evening, Hannah walked out the hospital emergency room doors with a rumpled, grass-stained Guthrie at her side. The sun had crept into bed for the night. Wispy clouds fluttered across a full moon, making it appear to wink at her.

Pausing, Hannah glanced at the hospital where she'd insisted on taking both her father and Guthrie to be checked out.

"You don't want to leave your parents," Guthrie rumbled sympathetically. Kindness filled his gaze.

She looked at him. "I didn't come to town to give my dad a heart attack."

"You *didn't* give him a heart attack. The doctor just wants to keep him overnight for observation. Your mom's staying with him. He'll be fine."

The man's rough sympathy did her in. Tears suddenly spilled down one of her cheeks. Just one. *I can't even cry right today!*

"You're not going to cry, are you?" He put his hands out as if she might break apart and he'd be expected to catch the pieces. Evidently feminine tears scared Guthrie more than falling off a roof.

A sob caught in her throat and became a giggle. "Oh, stop it. I refuse to cry." She wiped her moist cheek with her hand. "Let's go." She walked firmly to her red car and stretched out her hand to open the door.

A long arm reached around her. "I'll drive. You look upset."

"*You're* the one who fell off the roof. I'm perfectly capable of driving us home."

"Are you sure?" He hovered beside her.

Overwhelmed with his nearness, she waved toward the other side of the car. "Get in the passenger seat. I'm driving." She unlocked the door and got in. He followed suit. She drove away without another word.

Petite was only an eight-mile drive north of Portage. Good health-care facilities weren't available in every rural community. But fortunately, Petite Portage was close to an excellent medical center in the bigger town of Portage. That had been one of the reasons her parents had felt safe in moving from Milwaukee, which had several excellent hospitals, to Petite Portage. Last year, good health care had become very important to both Mom and Dad.

As she drove through the quiet streets to the highway north, she became more and more aware of the handsome man beside her. The scent of honest perspiration and freshly mowed grass floated in the air. He filled the vehicle, which had seemed so large to her after years of driving her little VW Beetle. "He's certainly big enough," she muttered to herself.

"What?"

Blushing, she turned onto the highway. "Nothing. I'm sorry you had to spend the whole evening being X-rayed and whatever."

"Poked and prodded?" He offered.

"Yes, it couldn't have been pleasant." Hannah thought ruefully that the nurses had been eager to help, however! At one time, three nurses had hovered around Guthrie while only one treated her father. Evidently, the nursing staff had agreed with Doree's assessment—"blonde, muscles, wow!"

He shrugged. "It turned out okay. I'm just bruised and a little stiff. Doc says a few days taking ibuprofen and I'll be fine."

"It's amazing you weren't hurt seriously." Hannah knew God's hand must have broken Guthrie's fall. The doctor had called him the luckiest man in Wisconsin.

"Well, the ground was wet, really soaked, from three days of rain. When Orville Jenkins mowed the lawn, I guess he dumped all the clippings in that pile because he was in a hurry."

"Fortunately." Hannah heaved a ragged sigh. Her emotions had run the gamut today. She felt peculiar, not herself.

"Yeah. You know I wouldn't have let your father come on the roof. I was just getting ready to come back in."

"I know. I believed you the first time. And it's just like my father to want to help someone."

"He's a great guy. We were lucky to get him as our pastor." Guthrie moved his seat back a little farther and stretched his legs in front of him.

She nodded, trying to keep her gaze off his long blue-jeaned legs and on the road. "Have you ever had a day where nothing went the way you planned?"

He snorted. "How about a whole summer? This has been the worst building season I've ever had. All the rain has been a real kick in the head. I got a late start as it is on your parents' contract, but I wasn't able to even pour your parents' foundation till July."

Hannah couldn't help herself. "What were you doing up on the church roof? On such a nice day, I would think you would be working on the house."

Hannah prepared herself to hear a long list of excuses, knowing she couldn't scold him.

"Didn't your parents mention the problem with the church roof?" Guthrie stretched his arms overhead toward the back seat and gave a little growl in the back of his throat.

That little sound shook her up, made her aware of him being so near. Why? "What roof problem?"

He lowered his arms and folded them in front of his chest. "All the rain in June destroyed what was left of the old roof. I've had to strip all the layers of old shingles off. Six layers, one layer too many. Now

I've begun replacing sections of the roof itself. I'll also have to replace some of the joists and beams in the church attic and the steeple."

"Can't someone else do that work?" Though the traffic on the road ahead was light, she concentrated intently on her driving. Ignoring the man beside her had become hard work.

"Sure, but the church wanted me to do it. I guess because my family helped build the first roof on the church a hundred years ago."

"And my parents agreed?" *Why am I asking him this? I already know their answer.*

"Of course." Guthrie shifted in his seat, making a subtle swishing sound on the leather.

Of course, her parents would agree. They would never make a fuss. Or put their needs before the church's needs. Hannah stared at the road. Another question slipped through her disobedient lips. "Why didn't you hire more help if you had two jobs to do?"

"Hire someone? I have a few guys that help me out when I need them, but they all have regular day jobs. I don't build enough to keep anyone else busy. I build houses and raise dairy cattle. So I usually only build one or two homes a year."

"I see." The words she'd wanted to say to him earlier came out. "My parents' contract says this house is to be completed by August thirty-first." She bit her lower lip.

He gave her a lopsided grin. "I just hope I can get the church roof done and your parents' home framed in before snow flies."

His calm tone ignited a spark of temper. "Framed in, not even completed before snow flies? Are my parents supposed to stay at Hanson-Fink's Cozy Motel for four more months? My parents have to be in a house before then!" Shocked at her outbreak, she swallowed. For a moment, she'd forgotten she'd scared this man off a roof.

Evidently, her outburst didn't faze him. "I know. I've told them over and over I'd tear up the contract. They should look into a factory-built home."

Turning off the highway, Hannah glanced at him with disbelief. His golden hair gleamed in the moonlight. "You offered to tear up their contract?"

"Yes, but they wouldn't hear of it."

The next afternoon, Hannah walked out of the hospital beside her parents into afternoon warmth and sunshine. After waiting four hours for one more test to be done, then a doctor to release her father, she felt like the proverbial cat on a hot tin roof. But a guilty, ineffective cat, she thought as they got into her car.

"I see you bought yourself a new car," Dad said.

She focused on the surface topic, pushing down the bubbling confusion inside her. "The old VW bought the farm in July. I thought a sport utility vehicle would be good for winter driving."

"And such a nice bright red," her mother remarked. "You'll be visible in any weather. How long are you going to be able to stay, Honey?"

Hannah swallowed. She couldn't stand to be called

that name, not after Edward had used it to belittle her.
Honey, you don't know what you're talking about.
"Mom, Dad, I'd like to ask you a favor. I would
really appreciate it if we could do away with Honey."

There was a pause. Then Dad cleared his throat.
"You've grown up, been that way a long time. If you
want to leave that childhood nickname in the past, no
problem. Right, dear?"

"Certainly. I may forget, so please remind me,"
Mom agreed.

Hannah felt foolish making a point of this, but she
needed to draw a line between the old Honey and the
new Hannah. Her parents had noticed the clothes she
was wearing, a pair of designer chinos in royal blue
and a blue-and-white-striped pima cotton T-shirt. But
they were too polite to make a big deal about her
change into colorful clothing. She suddenly had the
impression that they both thought she was a bomb
that might explode if handled roughly. It wasn't a
comfortable feeling.

"So, Hannah, when do you have to be back in
Milwaukee?" her mother asked.

"I don't have to go back. I sublet my apartment
for the rest of the lease." Her eyes on the road, Hannah sensed her parents' uneasiness. She knew them
so well, she could hear their unspoken questions to
each other. *Does this have to do with her breakup
with Edward? Is she having some kind of crisis? Does
she mean to move in with us? What's going on? How
can we help her?*

Tears caught in Hannah's throat. Ever since that

dreadful day two months after her breakup with Edward, the day she'd experienced shattering embarrassment, tears came out of nowhere whenever they wanted to. Gripping the steering wheel and refusing to give in, she drove onto the two-lane highway, concentrating on the scenery. But fields of ripe corn and pastures dotted with huge green rolls of drying hay and black-and-white dairy cattle didn't distract her.

The feeling that the three of them were holding hands, like children playing ring-around-a-rosy while circling an untouchable topic, hit Hannah. But she still couldn't broach what had happened *after* she had broken up with Edward. After the endless three-year engagement, just the breakup had been hard enough on her parents. She couldn't tell them the rest. It would break their hearts.

"Then what are your plans?" Dad asked.

"Nothing drastic." *That's already happened to me.* "I plan to help you two move into your new home. I'd like to get acquainted with your new church. Then I might go back to Milwaukee or see if I like the Madison area instead."

Dad cleared his throat. "There's something that we need to tell you, Hannah." He paused. "Our new home isn't going to be ready on time."

Hannah let out a deep sigh. "I know. I drove by your…foundation yesterday before I came to the church."

Dad breathed what sounded like a sigh of relief. "The wet weather all summer and spring has held Guthrie up."

"Guthrie explained that to me last night when I drove him home." She recalled the pleasant sensation of having Guthrie with her in this car. She gripped the steering wheel tighter. A dreamy feeling affected her as she recalled Guthrie sitting beside her. Obviously being on the rebound made her more susceptible than usual to a handsome man. That could only mean danger to her already mangled heart and pride!

Mom spoke from the back seat. "We think a lot of Guthrie."

Hannah replied in an even tone. "He seems like a nice guy. I mean he doesn't plan on suing me for causing him to fall off the roof yesterday. He didn't really even seem angry with me." He'd been sweet through it all. Some woman had raised one fine son.

"Guthrie Thomas is a special young man," Dad agreed.

Hannah heard the unspoken words. *Not like Edward who never appreciated you.*

"Guthrie mentioned that he was working on the church roof, too," Hannah said. Her parents were right. Guthrie and Edward had nothing in common except making Hannah wait!

Dad finished with, "Yes, the church has sustained water damage. It's really quite serious. Things had been neglected too long. The work couldn't be put off any longer."

Hannah added, "Guthrie told me that he didn't mind if you broke the contract with him."

"Yes, that was very thoughtful," Mom said soothingly.

"He mentioned he thought you should go with the company that makes factory-built homes," Hannah added without much conviction.

"Yes, he told us all about them." Beside her, Dad gazed out the window, looking unperturbed.

Hannah said brightly, but without hope, "So? Which company are you going to go with?"

"Why, none, Hannah. We'll just wait for Guthrie." Mom's placid voice floated forward.

Hannah made one last attempt. "Mom, he really sounded like he wouldn't be upset if you changed your minds."

"But we haven't changed our minds," Dad said as expected.

I don't believe this; then again, I knew just how this would go. "But your house might not be done for months. You don't want to stay at Fink's, I mean Hanson's Cozy Motel through the winter, do you?"

"Why not?" Mom asked, sounding tickled by some unspoken joke.

"Your mother is enjoying a welcome break from entertaining and housekeeping." Dad glanced over his shoulder with a smile in his eyes.

"Yes," Mom agreed, "it's a dream come true. No cleaning. Just making a snack at lunchtime. We even have dish-network TV," her mother added.

"But aren't you feeling crowded in just one room?" Hannah already felt cramped.

But her parents both chuckled.

"It reminds us of our first efficiency apartment

where we lived while your father attended the seminary." Then her mother frowned.

Just the word *seminary* had brought the specter of Edward into the car. Edward had refused to juggle working and studying at the seminary with marriage. So stupid little Honey had pushed ahead the wedding date and waited.

"Only this bathroom is larger," Dad said.

Hannah felt the sensation of trying to cross a bog. Every time she tried to move forward, sticky, unstable mud sucked her backward. "I give up. What's so special about waiting for a house Guthrie Thomas builds?"

"When we were deciding whether or not to take this pastorate, we took a long time to think it over," Dad said.

"We wanted this to be where we semiretired, so we had to make the right decision," Mom added.

"I can understand that, but—" Hannah tried once more, against all odds.

"Hon—Hannah," Dad interrupted, "your mother has never complained about the little efficiency apartment we started out in or the old drafty-barn parsonages that we lived in when you children were being born—"

"Garner, I never minded—"

"Ethel, I think our daughter needs to hear this. When a man marries a woman, he longs with all his heart to provide a castle worthy of her. In thirty-five years of marriage, I've never been able to do that." He cleared his throat. "Starting early this year, we spent several months deciding whether or not to take this pastorate. Then we spent a month looking for just the right lot. After that, we looked over hundreds of floor plans until we decided on the one that had everything we wanted. Finally we toured model homes of every kind in the area.''

Ethel took over. ''We decided on Guthrie Thomas, right in Petite. He does the most beautiful workmanship. Little touches like arched doorways and built-in cabinets, carved moldings. His houses are perfection!''

Garner nodded. ''This is probably the last house we will live in before we begin downsizing, when we get too old to keep up a full-size house and yard. That's why I insist that your mother get the house she wants. She's waited long enough. God has promised us a mansion in heaven, and I don't doubt it will be magnificent. But this is *my* last chance to give your mother the house I've always wanted for her, the one she's always deserved. And I won't be denied!''

Hannah loved every single word her father said, but she sighed anyway. It was a beautiful sentiment, but she had to think of something she could do to move matters along. Perfection could take a long time!

Chapter Three

Feeling like a lump of dough with sadly inactive yeast, Hannah lay on her double bed in her harvest gold and avocado green "box" at Fink-Hanson's Cozy Motel. After bringing her parents home, she'd tried to write her column, but had ended up, stretched out on her bed, staring at the ceiling. She'd come to Petite with a simple task, simply to help her parents move into their new home, maybe to hurry the local builder along with the finishing touches.

"Finishing touches," she moaned to the ceiling. At the back of her mind, her conscience reminded her she had to fax her column in before tomorrow. Column? She hadn't even written a word yet, hadn't even thought of a topic! She had never been late for a deadline in her life. Even this didn't stir her to action.

The bedside phone rang. Four rings jingled before Hannah had the energy to pick it up. "Hi."

"Hannah? Is that you?"

"Spring?" Hannah's eyes opened wide.

"Yes, it's me."

"Oh, Spring, it's so good to hear your voice," Hannah said.

"What's the matter?"

Images from yesterday flashed through Hannah's mind, Lila Fink, Captain Peach-fuzz, Guthrie Thomas sliding down the roof. "Oh," Hannah wailed, "I've entered the twilight zone!"

"What?"

Hannah sat up. "Yesterday was a once-in-a-lifetime nightmare! Nothing has gone like I planned!"

Spring had the nerve to chuckle! "Hannah, the busy planner."

"Don't make fun of me!"

"Life isn't a recipe you plan, measure out, then cook. It's time you realized that."

Hannah ran her fingers through her mussed hair. "Don't lecture me either. You're not here on the front line."

"What's the matter? Is the builder a hard nut to crack?"

Hannah pictured again Guthrie wiping grass clippings off his face. Later on the ride home, his grin had made her anger with him melt away. Now she didn't know if she felt like laughing or crying. "The house is just a foundation."

"What!"

"You heard me," Hannah grumbled.

"Why?"

Hannah explained the facts of the situation, then

finished, "But the kicker is the builder has told them he would let them out of the contract whenever they want."

"He what? Is he for real?"

"Yes, he meant it." Hannah stood up and walked to the window. The Front Street business district stretched before her, Carlson's Auto Repair, the Kwi-kee Gas station-convenience store and the Bizzy Bee Beauty Shop.

"Then...what's the problem?"

"Mom and Dad insist they want him to do it any-way!" Hannah had lost all her starch. She slumped into the straight chair at the small desk.

"What are you going to do then?"

Hannah sighed. "I wish I knew." Glancing at the clothes hanging against the wall, she shook her head. She'd brought a designer wardrobe for Petite. Now her new fashionable clothes mocked her.

Spring went on, "Well, if Mother and Father are convinced that this is what they want, there doesn't seem much you can do. Maybe you should just leave. You can always come back and stay with me if you need a place for a few weeks."

"I'm not ready to give up yet, but..."

"Have you done any more thinking about what we talked over at lunch?" Spring's voice became uncer-tain.

"You mean about finding Mother's adoption pa-pers?" Hannah felt a twinge of fear. *Mother, what should I do? Obey you or do what's best for you?*

"Yes."

"I'm still trying to decide, but what I think right now isn't very important. All Mom and Dad's stuff is in storage. And until they can get into their new home—"

"That's where it will stay." Spring paused. "If you need backup, just call me. I can get away from the Gardens with a day's notice."

"Thanks. But I don't see anything you could do here." Hannah paused, then perked up. "Oh! A thought just occurred to me."

"What?" Spring sounded excited.

"I'll tell you if it works."

"All right. Keep in touch. Love you."

"Love you, too. Bye."

At five that evening, Hannah walked between her parents down the crumbling sidewalk of Front Street, then turned up Church Street. They'd been invited to eat supper with Guthrie's family. Hannah hoped meeting Guthrie with his family wouldn't be awkward. She still felt embarrassed about the roof incident. What must they think of her?

"You'll love Martha, dear," Mom said. "She is so warmhearted."

"A good cook, too." Dad grinned. "Not quite up to your mother's standards, but good."

Hannah listened as her parents teased each other. The thought that had come to her as she'd talked with Spring that afternoon had rolled around in her mind ever since. She didn't think this would work, but she had to try it. She'd talk to Guthrie. He might agree. He might.

"Martha Thomas's daughter's name is Lynda Garrett."

"Yes." Hannah was used to her mother priming her with social details.

"Lynda's children are Amber, Jenna and Hunter. They are six, five and four."

"She's got her hands full! What's her husband's name?"

Dad spoke. "That's the unfortunate part. Lynda's husband deserted them just after Hunter was born."

"How awful!" At least, Edward had figured out he didn't want her before they were married.

"Yes. After that, Martha moved into town to live with her daughter and help out. But Lynda is wonderful. She's earned an associate degree at the community college and has just gotten a job as an executive assistant."

"I'm glad." Hannah concentrated on recalling all the names she'd just heard—Martha, the mom, Lynda, the daughter, Amber, Jenna, and Hunter, the kids. Would she have a chance to talk to Guthrie alone?

They arrived at the Thomas home, a small yellow house, and walked to the front door. A little blond girl in braids and red shorts waited at the door to the large screened-in porch. She squealed, "Grandma, they're here!" She swung the door wide open and launched herself into Garner's waiting arms.

He caught her. "Hi, pumpkin, what's for supper?" He planted a noisy smooch on the little girl's cheek.

Nostalgic longing swirled through Hannah. She remembered when Dad had called her pumpkin and given her noisy kisses. In those days, he had always been able to solve every problem, soothe every fear. Hannah brought herself back to the present. Her parents needed her help now, and she wouldn't fail them.

"Jenna, this is our middle daughter, Hannah." Dad nodded.

"Hi." Two huge brown eyes stared at her.

"Hi." Hannah grinned.

Mom held the door open, and Hannah stepped inside, followed by her parents. A rush of greetings and introductions took place, and soon they all sat on the porch with glasses of iced tea in hand. A second little girl with short, dark hair, Amber, sat in her grandmother's lap while blond Hunter played with a large plastic toy truck on the floor.

Martha, sitting across from Hannah, didn't look anything like Hannah had expected. A slender woman, Martha wore stylish navy slacks and a plaid oxford short-sleeve shirt and pretty leather sandals. Her golden hair, threaded with silver, had been cut in an easy care but attractive style.

"Mrs. Thomas." Hannah took a deep breath. "I want to apologize for yesterday—"

"Call me Martha and don't give that another thought. Guthrie needs a good shaking up from time to time. You'll meet my daughter soon. Lynda will be here in a few minutes. She called just before she left the office." Martha stroked Amber's back.

"Do you have any other children?" Hannah asked.

"Yes, my oldest, Brandon, is a lawyer in San Francisco."

Hannah nodded politely.

"Will Guthrie be coming to supper?" Mom asked.

Hannah listened for the answer. Would she have to face him in front of his family and be expected to eat?

"Who knows?" Martha grinned as though this were a perennial question. "I always serve dinner at six. Those who show up for it get it fresh. Those who don't..." She finished by lifting one hand, then gave an easy grin.

Garner chuckled as he glanced at his wife. "That's what you should have done."

"If I had," Mom replied with mock severity, "you would never have eaten a fresh meal."

"Guilty as charged." Dad tickled Jenna, who squealed with delight.

Martha looked at Hannah and asked, "I hear you are a food writer?"

"Yes, my Real Food, Healthy Food column appears in twelve papers now across the Midwest."

"Wonderful. I hear you've written two cookbooks already, too."

Blushing, Hannah nodded. "I see you've been talking to my parents." A door slammed, and the three children suddenly went on alert.

"Guthrie?" Martha called.

Hannah waited for the answer, breathless.

"It's me, Mom!" a feminine voice replied.

"That's Lynda," Martha said.

Hannah didn't know if she was relieved or disappointed.

Within moments, a thin young woman, very much like Martha, stepped onto the porch. Her children mobbed her. She kissed her daughters' heads, then swung Hunter into her arms. "Hello, rug rats!"

A touch of envy stung Hannah. If she and Edward had married right after college like she'd wanted, she could have been a mother by now. *A divorced single mother,* a bitter voice added. Edward had never been eager to become a parent. *That should have warned me off. How could I have been such a fool?*

After greetings and introductions had been accomplished, they all went to their places around a long picnic table on the wraparound porch.

A light tapping on the porch door caught Hannah's attention. She glanced over to see two slender older ladies standing on the top step.

"It's the great-aunties!" Jenna shouted and ran with blond braids flying to let them in.

"Hello!" Martha greeted them. "You're just in time for dinner."

Hannah watched Lynda welcome the two older women who wore identical pink-flowered dresses, which might have been new in 1965.

Martha looked at Hannah. "These ladies are my late husband's twin aunts, Ida and Edith Thomas."

Hannah exchanged greetings with the women, who reminded her of two of the actresses in a recent production of *Arsenic and Old Lace* she'd seen at a community theater in the spring. These two ladies could easily have played the aging sisters who were quietly poisoning lonely old men. Ida wore her silver hair pulled into a topknot, but soft bangs framed her cheerful face.

Edith's hair had been cut short and curled around her face into gentle waves. Edith was the same height but a bit rounder than her sister.

When everyone was seated, Hannah's father said a brief prayer, then Martha began to pass bowls family-style. The menu was the classic spaghetti with marinara sauce, salad and garlic bread.

Hannah tasted the tangy red sauce, chunky with tomatoes, onion and green pepper. "This is delicious!"

"It's just spaghetti sauce." Martha's cheeks turned pink. "Cooking for a food writer made me nervous, but I decided to go ahead and make the meal I'd planned for your parents."

"That's Mom's own recipe," Lynda said proudly. "She cans it herself."

"I don't wish to contradict you, Lynda," Ida said, "but this is our recipe. We gave it to your mother when she first married dear Randall. May he rest in peace."

"Absolutely," Edith commented.

Martha turned pinker. "Yes, of course, you've given me so many of your excellent recipes."

Martha and her daughter exchanged glances, then they both gave Hannah an uneasy look.

"Do you can a lot of this?" Hannah asked, puzzled. Had the great-aunts given her the recipe or not?

"No, I used to can almost one hundred quarts of tomatoes every summer and freeze bags and bags of sweet corn and green beans. But no more. Now I spend one day canning just tomatoes, then a day making spaghetti sauce and one day for salsa."

Hannah wiped her mouth with her napkin. "Is the salsa also your own recipe?"

This time neither aunt claimed the salsa as their own.

"Yes." Martha finished tying a bib around squirming Hunter's neck.

"I can see and taste that I'll have to get to know you better." Hannah grinned.

"Yes, Martha is a wonderful cook!" Ida and Edith chorused.

Martha glowed with honest pride, then she humbly changed the topic. "I guess Guthrie was unable to get away from work. I'll have to fix a dish for you to take to him, Lynda."

Her pulse sped up, and Hannah raised her hand. "I'll take it out to him."

"Oh, no." Martha objected.

"Please, it's the least I can do for him after scaring him off the roof yesterday!" *Besides, I have something to discuss with Guthrie.*

Nervous but determined, Hannah parked her fiery red sport utility vehicle on her parents' muddy gravel track. She opened the door and got out to deliver the covered nine-by-thirteen-inch pan Martha had filled with supper. She stepped gingerly on the mud-mired grass, then onto the path of boards toward the building in progress. She hummed "Onward Christian Soldiers" loudly so she wouldn't take Guthrie by surprise a second time.

"I hear you!" Guthrie called cheerfully. "Let me guess—that's your favorite song!"

His easygoing humor tickled her, made her feel alive. "No," she teased, "but do you smell your supper?"

"It's Mom's spaghetti and garlic bread. I'm starving!"

"Then you should have come home!"

Guthrie was shirtless again. Hannah dragged her eyes away from the bronzed picture he made in the golden twilight. Didn't the man know what the sight of him did to her knees?

"Sit with me while I eat?" he invited.

Still keeping her gaze away from the visual feast he offered, she sat on a hard, sharp-edged stack of lumber, leaving a chaste two-foot gap between them. "Okay. Get busy and eat before it's completely cold."

Guthrie used the wet wipes his mother had sent to clean his large, work-roughened hands. He sat beside her, took the pan onto his lap and bowed his head for grace.

Hannah bowed her head also, praying for guidance in this situation. The crickets of fall were already singing. Warm breezes whispered against her nose and earlobes.

"Amen," Guthrie murmured.

The sound of the word brought tears to Hannah's eyes. *I'm becoming a cry baby. I cry over everything.* Hannah blinked away the moisture. Ever since that day two months after the breakup, when Edward's sister had called to prepare her in case someone mentioned his wedding. She drew in a deep breath and began talking away the blues. "Two days without rain in a row. Think this might be the beginning of a trend?"

"I hope so. This summer has been frustrating."

I've had better summers myself. "I believe you. How much work do you have left on the church roof?" she asked, trying to get the facts she needed.

"I checked things over today. I'm waiting on an order for some joists, beams and wallboard to repair water damage in the attic. After I replace all the damaged roof boards, all I have left to do is replace some of the siding on the steeple, then I can start the shingling."

"Good."

"So today I worked on your parents' house, so you can see." He waved a slab of fragrant garlic bread toward the foundation. He'd been working on floor joists. For one man, he'd accomplished quite a bit in one day. Why did he insist on working a job alone?

Not voicing this concern, she bowed her head as if scolded. "I noticed. Here I was trying to be polite by not bringing this up."

He chuckled.

She looked at him sideways. His golden hair was damp from hard work. A fine layer of sawdust frosted his curls. She nearly reached over to fluff his hair and shake off the pale particles. "I like your family."

"Imagine that. I do, too." He tore off a hunk of the garlic bread.

Trying to come up with some safe newcomer-type subject, she asked, "What is there to do for fun around here?"

"Fun? You want to have fun, Miss Hannah?"

The rich coaxing tone he used made the hair on the back of her neck prickle. "If I decide to hang around."

"I thought you were just here to make sure that your parents got into their house on time." Guthrie twisted saucy spaghetti around his fork.

"That's true." No sense mincing words, then. "Guthrie, you said that you have offered to let my parents out of their contract. Did you mean that?"

He swallowed his swirl of spaghetti. "Yes."

"Then I was wondering if you would take it a step further." Hannah stretched her legs and gazed at the fading sunlight.

"How do you mean that?" Guthrie took a drink from a quart jar of iced tea.

"Would you tell them *you'd* like to break the contract?" She held her breath even though she could almost predict his answer.

He stared at her. "But that would be a lie. I don't want to break the contract."

She hung her head, discouraged. "That's what I expected you to say. In fact, I agree with you."

"Hannah, your parents may be semiretiring, but

they are still competent adults. At the very beginning, I explained to them that I work mostly alone with little help. We discussed the possibility of weather causing delays. As of yesterday, they still wanted me to build their home.''

She nodded. ''I know. You are the builder they want to build their dream house.'' She hadn't fully realized that before, but she did now.

''Then why do you want them to settle for a factory-built house?'' He began twisting his fork again, gathering another tangy mouthful.

She gave him a rueful smile. ''I don't, really. I just thought it was important for them to get into their home as soon as possible. They may say they don't mind staying at the Cozy Motel, but it will cease to be a novelty in the next few weeks.''

Guthrie nodded.

Leaning backward, she looked at the endless twilight sky—golden bands between slate-blue layers. ''My sister called today and laughed at me. Called me Hannah, the planner, and told me I couldn't treat life like a recipe.''

''What?''

''Oh, nothing, but...'' Mom's leukemia was certainly something. She didn't want to take her mother's return to health for granted. And her sisters' idea of looking for Mom's adoption papers lurked in the back of her mind, lending urgency to the need to get her parents settled. What to do?

Pushing away these concerns, she turned to face him. ''I really want to help my parents with this move. They've had health problems crop up in the past year, and I wanted this to go smoothly.''

"I can see that."

"I'm not licked yet. I want my parents in their dream house before snow flies and I will find a way."

He shook his head. "Well, be sure to let me know what you come up with. I'll be interested."

"Don't worry. You'll be the first to know."

Sitting with her black laptop in her lap, Hannah rubbed her eyes. The bedside clock read one a.m. She ran the spell-check on her computer, then connected the jack and cord between the computer and phone. She quickly set up the fax information and tapped "Enter."

"Goodbye," she murmured as her column, "Old and New Canning Recipes and Tips," traveled through the phone lines to her newspapers. With a groan, she laid down on her bed. She yawned and whispered a good night prayer....

The blare of a trucker's horn woke her. She sat up. Thin, early sunlight sifted through blinds into her room. The images in the dream she'd awakened from sent a thrill through her. The memories must be an answer to prayer. *Thank you, Lord. Now I know what I can do.*

Chapter Four

Several hours later at nearly ten on another cloudy morning, Hannah swung into the church parking lot and with a quick spin of the wheel parked her red SUV beside Guthrie's sky-blue pickup. Aha! When she'd driven by her parents' lot and found it uninhabited, she'd known she'd find Guthrie here.

Right after breakfast at the Cozy Café, she'd driven to the Farm and Fleet out on the highway and bought heavy-duty overalls and tan work boots. Then she went to her room, tore off the tags and pulled on the stiff denim. Finally, she'd wiggled her cotton-socked toes in the steel-toed boots making sure she had enough toe room.

She was ready. She was set. It was a go!

Saying a quick prayer, she grabbed her red plastic toolbox, climbed out of the vehicle and jogged through the side door leading into the church basement.

Her mother was speaking on the phone in the church's outer office. No doubt her father sat in the inner office hard at work preparing Sunday's sermon. *I'm doing this for you, Mom and Dad. You need to get settled and the sooner the better.* Mom's remission and her sisters' suggestion that Hannah look for Mom's birth documents nipped at the back of her mind, but Hannah waved and went on. Hammering from above beckoned her irresistibly.

The church was so small it wasn't difficult to find the short flight of tan-painted steps that led her to the main floor, then to the narrow, dark-wood staircase and attic. The pounding became louder with each step. And each step lifted her spirits. Since she'd arrived in Petite, she'd been mired in a bog of disappointment.

Today that had changed! She bubbled inside with happy purpose. Arriving in the attic, she breathed in the welcome scent of fresh-cut wood.

Guthrie's back was to her as he crouched, pounding replacement boards over floor joists. He hadn't heard her approach. She opened her mouth to say something, then paused to watch as he hammered. The muscles of his back rippled under the taut white T-shirt.

No doubt about it. Guthrie Thomas was a masterpiece of a man. When God had crafted this carpenter's genes, He'd been extravagantly generous. But God Himself had chosen to be born into a carpenter's family. Maybe He had a soft spot for them.

Guthrie's every move was sure and strong, without

hesitation or fumbling. But something, some thought she'd had about Guthrie in her late-night deadline session last evening eluded her now. She creased her forehead, thinking. *Yes!*

"Why aren't you married?" The words popped out of her mouth.

Guthrie shot up and spun around. "Hannah!"

She covered her hot face with her hands. "I'm sorry." After three years of holding back her true feelings so she wouldn't upset Edward, she'd lost control of her tongue. Now words she'd never dreamed of saying aloud would pop out of her mouth. *I hope this goes away—and soon!*

"Why did you sneak up on me like that?" He put down his hammer.

"I know! I'm sorry!" She didn't blame him for being exasperated with her, but she hoped he hadn't heard her question. How embarrassing!

Experience had taught her that whenever a woman mentioned marriage near a man, he thought she was interested in him. If he only knew! Marriage should be the last thing on her mind. Besides, Guthrie could give any leading man competition, and she was just plain old Hannah. But why hadn't he married a high school sweetheart and started a family by now? That was the mystery!

Bending his head under a low rafter, he stepped closer to her. "What can I do for you?"

He must not have caught her question, and he wasn't angry over her startling him again. His calm words and manner showed this. Easygoing Guthrie.

Trying to ease her stress, she shrugged her tense shoulders to relax them. "Nothing. I mean, I came...." Her words petered out. How would Guthrie Thomas take to her idea?

In her rush to get rigged out and in the excitement of finally coming up with some positive action, she'd ignored a fluttering in the back of her mind, a touch of concern over how Guthrie would like her plan.

He paused, eyeing her. "I need to keep at it. More showers are predicted today, so I gave up the idea of working on your parents' house. I've started to work here inside on the attic—"

She decided to say it and get it over with. "Guthrie, I finally thought of a way to help you get my parents' house done more quickly."

"Really? How?" He sauntered over to where he'd been hammering and squatted, his thigh muscles molding the well-worn denim.

"I'm going to work with you. Be your carpenter's helper."

He popped up like toast from a toaster. "What!"

She'd snagged his attention, all right. Would he proceed to opposition next? "Yes, I suppose you didn't know that I've done construction work."

"You? Construction?" He looked at her as though she were babbling nonsense.

She nodded. "I went on mission trips to Arkansas and Haiti."

"Mission trips? What has that got to do with building your parents' house?"

She anchored one hand on her hip. The other

gripped her toolbox. "I helped rebuild a church in Arkansas after a tornado destroyed it. In Haiti, I built small cement-block homes for the poor."

He took a step nearer. "This is not going to be a one-room cement-block—"

She lifted her chin. "I also helped build two Habitat for Humanity homes in Milwaukee."

He stopped and stared at her. "You're serious."

"Very serious. My parents need their house finished, and the sooner the better. The weather has delayed you. You're only one man. One person can only do so much." She waved two fingers in the air. "But two can do twice the work of one."

Looking nonplussed, he measured her with his gaze. "You're not strong enough. I mean, look at you."

His frank stare made her blush, so to hide this she looked at herself. What did he see? She was no ethereal angel like her sister Spring. Anyone could see she was built to work. She said in a determined tone, "They didn't seem to think I was too weak to do a day's work in Arkansas, Haiti and Milwaukee."

Guthrie pushed his hands through his golden hair. "This beats all." He grinned then. "This is really sweet of you, but I can't let you."

Giving him a confused look, she set her toolbox on a nearby sawhorse. "Why not?"

"You're a food writer, not a carpenter. Don't you think that will keep you busy enough?"

He's evading the issue. "Guthrie, I'm perfectly capable of helping you build my parents' house. Why don't you let me worry about whether I have enough time?''

"It's not right." He shoved his hands in his back pockets and looked down.

Imitating him, she shoved her hands in her back pockets and took a step closer to him. "It makes perfect sense, and I'm here to assist you with the church, too.''

"No." He shook his head. "It's just not right. I contracted to build your parents' house, and I can't have you working without being paid. But I can't afford to pay—"

"Seeing my parents in their home before Christmas will be my payment.''

He sucked in breath. "I don't know if the construction insurance would cover you.''

"Guthrie Thomas, you're grabbing at straws." Why did men react like this? Like women couldn't do he-man stuff, pound nails and work a saw? "Now let's get busy." In her stiff new work boots, she picked her way over the exposed floor joists to the sawhorse and opened her small toolbox. She turned to Guthrie expectantly.

"What's that?" He pointed to her red toolbox.

She felt like saying something sassy like, "I'll give you three guesses," but she suppressed it and said with a straight face, "I brought my own hammer and a few other tools. I've gathered a small collection of necessary items. I know how carpenters hate other people using their tools.'' She pulled out her hammer and hefted it in one hand. "Now let's stop talking and start working. How can I help with this floor?"

Guthrie stared at her as though she'd just spoken in Greek. He didn't move a muscle.

Tossing the hammer from one hand to the other, she walked as close to him as she could. "What job are we doing here today?"

With a decided frown, Guthrie folded his arms over his chest.

With a deceptive smile, Hannah folded her arms over her chest. *I'm not giving in, Guthrie Thomas. I let Edward overrule me for three years. Now you're stuck with me. This church and my parents' house are going to be finished and I'm going to help you.*

The sound of footsteps came from behind her. "Hannah!" her mother said. "I wondered why you were wearing overalls and work boots. You've come to assist Guthrie!"

From behind her mother, Hannah's father chimed in. "What a generous idea, daughter. We can always count on our Hon—our Hannah!"

Guthrie stared forlornly at the light rain trickling down the dirty, grease-smudged front window of Carlson's Auto Body and Repair. The garage was more than fifty years old, steeped in motor oil, dirt and gas fumes.

Under the hood of Guthrie's blue pickup, his life-long friend Ted Carlson twisted another cleaned spark plug into place. "So could she do the work or not?"

That morning Hannah had expertly measured and

cut the boards for him. They'd put the new floor in the attic in no time at all. But by the time they'd broken for lunch, Guthrie had been ready to explode. He swung around and growled, "That's not the point."

"Well, it's going to be. If she can do the work, it will probably turn out okay." Ted bent over the engine. "If she can't, you're in for it."

Guthrie looped his thumbs in his belt. "I work alone because I like to work alone." In his mind, he heard Hannah's startling question once again. "Why aren't you married?"

"Know what you mean. Feel the same way. But how can you tell her not to help when her parents think it's great? Isn't polite. He's the new preacher. Can't tell him off, or at least you shouldn't."

Guthrie leaned under the raised hood to watch Ted. "Tell me something I don't know." Why had she brought up his not being married, then gone on like she hadn't asked it?

"Well, I'll tell you this. Mr. Kirkland stopped by yesterday to introduce himself." Ted pulled out, then cleaned another spark plug with a metal brush. "Said he'd heard my dad had been a regular church attender till he died two years ago."

"Did he invite you to church?"

"Said he'd be glad to see me back on Sunday mornings. I said I like to sleep in on Sunday mornings. Wondered how he'd take that. Just laughed." Ted twisted the clean plug in.

"He's a good guy." Guthrie made himself concentrate on what Ted was saying. "I liked him right away. He's solid, not a fake."

"Asked me if I'd ever be interested in attending a singles' night at the church." Coming out from under the hood, Ted stared at the toes of his scratched work boots.

"What?"

"Said he was going to start a singles' night in the church basement once a month this fall. Snacks, country music, videos. Everything just casual. Come and spend the evening. Also said he'd like to get up some groups to go to some football games in Madison."

"College games?"

Ted nodded.

Guthrie wondered if these were the preacher's ideas...or Hannah's. "I don't want to hang around with a bunch of kids."

"Said the singles' nights would be for twenty-one and older. No teenyboppers."

Guthrie could see that Ted looked interested, and why not? Their little town had nothing to offer socially after high school for singles. Most of the marrying took place in the year or two after high school graduation. But in the eight years since Guthrie's graduation, those marriages had been breaking up at an unpleasant but steady rate. Just like his sister's had.

Ted and he hadn't followed the general practice. Ted had always been too shy. Had Ted ever guessed why Guthrie hadn't married? He wondered if that had anything to do with his not wanting Hannah Kirkland working beside him. He wasn't lucky in love. He liked Hannah so far. But had she come to town with marriage on her mind?

"Think your sister would be interested in going to a singles' night?" Ted nonchalantly wiped his hands on some gray-blue paper toweling.

"Might. Mom will probably encourage her to."

"Rain's stopping." Ted pointed outside.

Guthrie exhaled with relief. "It's time I got back to the church. I might get some work done on that steeple before supper."

Ted nodded. "See you. Maybe the preacher's daughter will work out."

Guthrie glared at his friend. "I'm not going to cut her any slack. If she wants to work, I'll let her. But I don't think she will be able to hack it."

"She may surprise you."

"*I* may surprise *her.*" He got into his truck and backed out of the garage, feeling as grumpy as a ten-year-old getting socks for Christmas. But not clear on why.

Guthrie found Hannah sitting innocently beside her mother in the church office in the basement. He nodded politely to Mrs. Kirkland. "Ready to do some work, Hannah?"

Looking perky, Hannah saluted him and stood up. "Reporting for duty, sir!"

He refused to be charmed. "Come on then. It's not raining, so I want to try to replace the flashing around the steeple before it starts again."

"Guthrie, you'll use the safety harness, won't you?" Hannah's mother cautioned.

He grinned, accustomed to maternal warnings. "No problem. My mother already reminded me this morning."

"We just don't want any more surprises," Mrs. Kirkland said apologetically.

"Then you might tell your daughter not to scream suddenly while I'm out on the roof." He kept his tone vaguely humorous. After all, Hannah hadn't intentionally scared him off the roof. He didn't want to be rude, but he didn't want Hannah working with him, either!

Hannah grinned. "Don't worry. As long as neither of my parents are on the roof, you won't hear a peep out of me."

He waved Hannah ahead of him. Without further conversation, he followed her as she trudged up the church steps to the attic. He tried to ignore the intriguing feminine swing of the denim blue overalls in front of him. Overalls shouldn't make a woman more attractive. It wasn't right!

In the attic, she turned to face him. "So what can I do to help you?"

"Flashing is the—"

"Is the covering applied wherever there is a joint on a roof. As the house settles, the flashing keeps any joints on the roof covered even if joints separate some. It's usually metal. I'm figuring this church is old enough to have lead instead of aluminum. Am I right?"

The easy flow of information knocked Guthrie for a loop. "Did Habitat for Humanity put you in charge of flashing?"

She grinned. "No, I just like to sound like I know what I'm doing."

Her brash candor teased him, easing the tenseness inside him. He almost smiled, but conquered it. He wouldn't let her push the advantage a pretty woman always had. He went on without emotion. "The old flashing is lead. I need to remove it and replace it with modern aluminum. I'll put on the harness and attach it to the steeple. You can sit up in the steeple opening and hand me out what I need."

"I'm not afraid of heights."

"Neither am I, but I'm the only one who's going out on the roof today." He pinned her with his intense gaze. "That tight area around the steeple won't allow two of us to work out there. You'd just get in my way." *Just like you are, anyway.*

She teased him with another saucy grin. "Whatever you say. You're the boss of this job."

And don't you forget it. He snapped on the brown leather harness. Sitting in the opening on the side of the steeple, he secured his harness rope. He backed out onto the shingleless roof and straddled its damp, slick peak. "Now use the tin snips to cut each piece the same length and hand me out one piece of step flashing at a time."

After he stripped the old flashing, Hannah offered him the first piece of silvery aluminum. He pounded a ninety-degree angle, then tapped and nailed the Lshaped piece snugly into place, bridging the gap where the steeple and roof met. Piece by piece, Guthrie worked away from the steeple opening until he reached the next side of the steeple, forcing Hannah to venture out to perch on the peak to feed the flashing to him.

"Now I don't want you to move from that safe spot. I want your feet inside the steeple," he ordered. He was standing with his feet braced against the roof. The harness around his midsection attached him safely to the steeple so his hands were free to work and his eyes were free to look at Hannah. He tried to ignore the way the breeze tousled and played with her walnut-toned hair.

"I wouldn't have it any other way." She waved a piece of flashing at him, and it made a funny wobbling whistle.

Replying with only a stare, he stonewalled her attempt to lighten the mood. He rarely felt grumpy, but her horning in on his territory had pushed him too far.

She appeared to ignore his dark mood. "I'm going to cut several pieces ahead, and when you get to the point where you're going to be on the side opposite me, I'll load you up before you move to that side away from me."

"Who did you say was the boss here?" He needled her.

"Just obeying orders. You don't want me crawling around to reach you, do you?"

"No!" He slammed a nail in hard.

"Then I'll get busy and cut extra pieces for you. You can tuck them into the front of your tool belt."

While waiting for Hannah to lean around to hand him the next piece of flashing, he gazed at the town below. The rain had left every lawn and tree a stunning green. The clouds had cleared off. The August sun warmed his shoulders, and he hoped it meant tomorrow would be a day he could do more outside work. Without Hannah's help.

Looking at the little yellow house where his mother and sister lived, he watched an unfamiliar battered silver truck drive up and park in front of it. Who was stopping there and why?

He tapped another piece of flashing into place and glanced down. He saw the stranger get out and head toward his sister's front door. Something about the man's build and walk stirred Guthrie's memory. It couldn't be, could it?

Chapter Five

Guthrie's mother handed him the fresh white dish-towel. She sent him one of those pointed looks, those looks mothers give sons when, out of the blue, they volunteer to dry the dishes, kind of her chin down and her eyes peering over her half glasses at him like he was a specimen in a test tube.

"What?" he asked. "What?"

"Nothing. I'm delighted to have help in the kitchen." Mom turned off the hot water and pulled on bright yellow rubber gloves.

"Well, I just thought you...would," he explained with a lame shrug.

She handed him a dripping Mickey Mouse glass warm from the scalding rinse water. "You were strangely quiet at supper tonight."

"Oh?" *Why don't you just tell me about the stranger in the silver truck, Mom? Was it Terri Sue's truck like I thought?* It was driving him nuts. He had to know! He looked back to find her staring at him.

"Guthrie, what is the problem?"

"Nothing's wrong," he fibbed to his mother. Why couldn't he just ask her?

"Then why are you just holding that glass? Why don't you try drying it?"

He caught the amusement in his mother's tone. "I had a kind of...rough day." He rubbed the glass dry, placed Mickey upside down on the cabinet shelf and accepted another.

"I thought you said you got some work done on the attic and roof."

"I had some unwelcome help."

"Grandma! Grandma!" Jenna, her braids flying, ran into the kitchen. "I finally finished my cake."

His mother accepted Jenna's chocolate-crumb-decorated saucer.

"Mommy's going to read us a story." The little girl started to run into the front room, then reversed and rushed back. "I love you, Uncle Guthrie! I'm glad you came to supper tonight! We missed you last night." For a split second, she wrapped her arms around his knees.

Guthrie's heart clenched, but before he could bend down and hug her, she raced out of the kitchen door, calling, "Don't start without me! I get to pick a story, too!"

He looked at his mother. This time she was the one with a preoccupied expression on her face. What was on her mind? Was it today's mystery visitor? Or something else?

"You're a good man, Guthrie. And you'll do what is right. I know that. I want you to remember that."

He couldn't think how to answer this, so he accepted the glass she was holding and glanced away. He made his voice brisk. "You won't believe this, but Hannah Kirkland worked as my carpenter's helper today."

"Hannah?" Mom scrubbed Hunter's bright blue tippy cup.

"That's what I said. I couldn't stop her."

"You couldn't?" His mother chuckled, then became serious. "I would think you'd welcome some help."

And I thought you'd tell me about the stranger in the silver pickup without my asking. "I like working alone."

"What did she do?" Mom handed him the rinsed plastic cup. "How did she do?"

The second question made him scowl.

"I know that look very well," his mother said in a teasing voice.

"What does that mean?"

"It means you're just like your father. You make up your mind and don't like people messing with your plans."

"What's wrong with that?" He upended the dry tippy-cup on top of one of the Mickey Mouse glasses.

She chuckled. "Life has a way of making a mess of some of our plans. Haven't you noticed? I never intended to be the wife of a stubborn farmer. I was studying to be an art professor. But I'm glad my plans got messed up. Aren't you?''

He scrutinized her. ''Why are you talking about marriage all of a sudden?''

''Because I think it's time you thought about it, talked about it, did it.''

''You've never said things like that before,'' he objected.

''I've been waiting patiently for you to do it without me saying anything.'' She offered him the first piece of pale green stoneware to dry.

Absently circling the plate with the towel, Guthrie tried to think of a reply. Marry? Didn't his mother understand that he intended to be the bachelor uncle? How could he ever take a chance on marrying?

Years ago, when his parents had gotten married, marriage had been for life. Now it seemed to last only as long as it proved convenient. A guy could marry someone and...bam! Have the rug yanked out from under him. Child support, custody—the very words chilled him. If he fathered a child, he wouldn't be able to bear being legally separated from that child. His nieces and nephew had taught him that. But hadn't divorce happened to about everyone he'd grown up with? Even his own beautiful, sweet sister.

His mom opened her mouth. ''Guthrie, I—''

''Martha, dear!'' A familiar sweet voice called from the screen door.

Guthrie closed his eyes. The great-aunts had arrived to scarf-up all the leftovers, as Amber would say.

"Ida, Edith, come in. Come in." His slim mother, dressed in faded jeans like the college girl she'd been when she'd married Dad, held open the screen door.

The aunts, wearing outdated dresses they'd probably sewn in the fifties, entered the kitchen. They must still have every dress they'd ever sewn or bought. Aunt Ida proudly held high a jar of sick-looking cucumbers. "We made pickles today."

Mom took the jar. "Oh, thank you. We have some stew left and chocolate cake. I hope you both have room for it."

Though the arrangement had never been discussed, Guthrie knew his mother always cooked extra. In the summer, the aunts dropped by. In the cold weather, Lynda or Guthrie carried food to their door.

The phone rang. Guthrie lifted the receiver. "Hi."

"Guthrie? This is Hannah. I'm sorry. Tomorrow I won't be able to work a full day...."

Aha! I was right! She won't last.

"I'm really kind of excited. I've done my food column for three years now, but I've never done a live cooking demo for TV. The Madison station that does on-the-scene interviews called my agent and asked if I could fill in for a noon cancellation." Her voice bubbled.

"Great!" Saved by a noon cancellation!

She giggled in his ear. The sound made his neck hair feel funny. "You're not off the hook, fella! I'll still be able to help out after the noon show. I mean, after I clean up my cooking mess in the church kitchen.''

''Is that where you'll be cooking?''

''Yes, since neither my mother nor I *have* a kitchen, as yet.'' She paused pointedly.

He felt the little pinch of the scold she'd meant for him. ''Okay! Okay!''

''Tell your mom and great-aunts to come to the demo if they want. They'd like a live audience. Dad's going to set up chairs in the basement.''

''Will do.'' The change in plans and the fact that Hannah wouldn't be working with him hit him funny. Why wasn't he happier?

''Okay then. See you tomorrow after lunch!''

''Who was that?'' his mother asked.

As Guthrie relayed Hannah's good news and her invitation to his mother and aunts, the image of Hannah sitting in the steeple opening earlier in the day with her short, walnut-colored hair fluttering in the breeze against the blue sky flashed in his mind.

The church basement was alight and a-buzz. Metal poles with racks of lights brightened the drab room. Fortunately, the basement kitchen, if not stylish, was neat and clean. A TV camera's black coils of thick wire snaked around the tan metal folding chairs, set up in four neat rows of ten across. Senior citizens primarily filled the chairs, along with a few mothers holding children on their laps. Sitting beside Martha with Hunter on her lap, Guthrie's great-aunts, wearing matching lavender dresses, circa 1966, sat primly in the front row. They waved at her.

She waved back and smiled. Then she realized she'd been searching the audience for Guthrie's handsome face. *Get real! He's on the roof shingling!*

"Now, Miss Kirkland, we've only got a few minutes to go, then we're on live." The producer of the crew, wearing a headset like some techno-tiara, asked, "Do you have everything ready?"

Hannah glanced at the precise plan she'd typed and nodded. "I've already prepared one casserole and have the ingredients to demonstrate one for the camera."

"Great! We really appreciate your filling in on such short notice." He glanced at his wristwatch. "You have three minutes, forty seconds. So just hit the highlights."

"I will." She took a deep breath.

"Good choice of outfit." He gestured toward her. "The solid red will be a good background to the green beans."

Thank you. I picked it out just for that reason. I saw it on the hanger and thought, Now, that shade of red will be a good background for green beans. She felt a bit slaphappy from nerves. Live TV. That meant no-mistakes-please TV. *Why did I think this would be a good idea?*

"Okay, here we go," the head of the TV crew announced to the audience. "Everyone, clap after I introduce Miss Kirkland and at the end. Otherwise, please stay still. Thank you."

The TV local-assignments reporter, wearing matching gray sport coat and slacks, took his place beside her in the kitchen and looked through the louvered opening into the fellowship hall.

The producer counted down. "Four, three, two, one." He pointed at the reporter.

"Hi, Jim Harue here, in tiny Petite Portage at the historic Petite Community Church. I'd like to introduce Hannah Kirkland who writes the syndicated column Real Food, Healthy Food for newspapers all over the Midwest."

On cue, the audience clapped. The reporter continued, "Ms. Kirkland—"

"Please call me Hannah." She smiled extra wide and felt like a fake.

"Hannah, what are you cooking for us today?"

"Well, Jim, this is the season of bounty. All the carefully tended gardens in central Wisconsin are pouring out tomatoes, zucchini and green beans, which is our topic today. This is the type of vegetable recipe that takes a traditional favorite, green beans with bacon, and gives it a new healthy twist. It's high in calcium and makes a great side dish to any grilled meat. Or it could be the heart of a delicious meal."

"What are the ingredients?"

"I start with six cups of fresh green beans, lightly steamed and drained." She held up a silvery aluminum colander with prepared green beans in it. "One cup of bread crumbs—"

The sound of two feminine voices and footsteps in the audience caught Hannah's attention, but she kept her mind on the recipe. "And four slices of crisp bacon, crumbled. Set these aside—"

"That's not the way this recipe goes," Guthrie's great-aunt Ida insisted. "I've made this for years and years. You don't need bread crumbs for bacon and green beans."

"Absolutely not," her sister Edith agreed. "Mother never made it that way."

The reporter beside Hannah froze, his eyes bugging out.

Hannah wondered if she wore the same expression. Her chest felt pinched. She had a hard time catching a breath.

"Ladies," Hannah said quickly, "I'm making a new recipe. Why don't you—"

"A new recipe? How marvelous!" Ida said.

"Oh, we can't miss that, then." Edith crowded close on one side of Hannah, forcing back the reporter. Ida hovered on the other side.

Hannah trained her eyes on the camera. *Oh, Lord, help me! This could be a disaster. What can I do but go on with the original plan?* "Now I...we will make the sauce."

"Oh, this is wonderful! She's going to make sauce!" Ida crooned around Hannah to Edith.

Edith applauded.

Everyone else applauded along with her. The reporter eased out of camera range.

Don't desert me now! Coward!

Hannah went on adhering to her plan. "Melt one-fourth cup of margarine and stir in one-half cup of chopped onions.'' She dolloped the premeasured margarine into a nonstick skillet, instantly producing a cheery sizzle. ''Sauté them lightly, then stir in—''

''I've never been able to digest onions, Hannah,'' Ida interrupted. ''They make me bilious.''

''Oh, that's right,'' Edith lamented with a sad shake of her silver head. ''Can we take out the onions, Hannah?''

''Of course you can.'' With a wooden spoon, Hannah womanfully stirred the aromatic margarine and onions. ''I'm stirring in four tablespoons of flour and two teaspoons of salt—''

''Oh, we'd have to take out the salt. We have high blood pressure, you know.'' Ida looked apologetic.

''You might use another favorite seasoning or a salt substitute,'' Hannah ad-libbed. ''Then you add plain low-fat yogurt and cottage cheese and a dash of pepper.''

The producer held up one finger, the signal that she had one minute to go. Feeling a bit light-headed, she said, ''Bring these to a nice bubble, then pour the sauce over the green beans and half the bread crumbs already in a casserole dish. Top with your favorite low-fat cheese, the rest of the bread crumbs and the crumbled bacon. You may substitute turkey for bacon if you wish, or delete the bacon for a vegetarian dish. Microwave for approximately ten minutes, and voilà!'' She bumped Ida's arm, but managed to lift the still warm prepared casserole.

''Oh!'' Ida and Edith crowed. ''It smells delicious!''

The reporter stepped into camera range. "Thanks so much, Hannah." He paused. "And ladies."

The sisters beamed at him.

He continued gazing fixedly at the camera. "The complete recipe is available on our Web site, shown at the bottom of your TV screen, or you may send us a self-addressed stamped envelope for a copy."

Hannah gave another bright smile to the camera. "Don't forget my latest cookbook, *Real Food, Healthy Food,* Volume two. It's available at any bookstore, or order it from my Web site."

The twin great-aunts led the audience in an enthusiastic finale of clapping.

Setting down the casserole with intense relief, Hannah stepped around the sisters to thank the reporter, the producer and the cameraman.

The demo had been a roller-coaster ride from start to finish. The crew said all that was polite but kept glancing sideways at the sisters. Her heart still palpitating in little jerks, Hannah accompanied the men through the church and outside.

Within minutes, the crew and reporter loaded their equipment and got into their white van, which sported a communication dish on its top. As the van drove away, Hannah waved one last time.

The two sisters led the rest of the audience out the front doors of the church. "Oh, that was fun!"

The happy seniors of Petite crowded around Hannah, congratulating her. Hannah nodded, shook hands and tried to put names with faces. Martha waved as she hurried away with Hunter.

Finally, only the sisters remained. "We're going to make that recipe this week and bring it to the potluck on Sunday," Ida said with a decided nod.

"Oh, yes. Of course, we might make a few bitty little changes." Edith giggled, and the sisters walked away still chattering with excitement.

Hannah plopped down on the church steps. Her mother sat beside her. They exchanged glances, which communicated a family motto—never a dull moment.

"A very interesting experience," her mother murmured. "But you handled it well."

They looked at each other again before bursting into laughter.

Evidently the aunts had taken her invitation as a request to be a part of the program. Hannah felt the tension drain out of her. *Well, God, thanks for an interesting experience. Thanks for keeping me humble.*

Nearly an hour later, wearing her brand-new safety harness over a pair of denim overall shorts and a buttery yellow T-shirt, Hannah scooted through the opening in the steeple. "Guthrie! I don't want to startle you again!" she shouted over the noise of his nailing. "Guthrie, I'm coming out!"

His hammering halted. "Hannah, I don't want you out on this roof!"

"Too bad. I'm out on it already!" Straddling the peak, she inched her way around until she faced him. Laughing with her mother over the "live-TV disaster'' earlier had brightened her mood. She grinned at him. "I'm an experienced roofer."

"Of course, you are!" he agreed with a sarcastic twist. "But I don't want you up here. It's too dangerous."

"Please, let's just drop this argument, okay? You'll never get the church and house done this year without help. Now, I've got on my safety harness, and it's hooked to the support." She jiggled it at him. "Plus I noticed the scaffold for shingles and the roof jacks you've put in place. I can see you've taken every precaution, and I won't take any chances, I promise!" She pulled on white cotton work gloves. "Now you just stick to your side of the roof, and I'll stick to mine."

"So much for me being the boss of this job!" Guthrie groused.

"I don't mind your deciding what work is to be done and how, but I think we've exhausted the 'sweet little Hannah doesn't know one end of the hammer from the other' routine—thank you very much!"

Guthrie growled at her. "For the record, I'm still against this! And I'm coming over to show you how to do this right. I don't want to waste time and good money ripping off perfectly good shingles!"

"Yes, Guthrie, of course, Guthrie!" She giggled, then let herself down the side of the roof, as if it were the side of a mountain, to the scaffolding that spanned this side of the roof. Yesterday had been gloomy. Today only cottony white clouds blocked the sun.

The bundles of green asphalt shingles had been delivered directly onto the roof. Guthrie appeared on the peak and looked at her. Before he could speak, she said, "Just watch me and see if I do it to suit you!"

He grunted suspiciously.

She ripped open the brown paper covering the nearest bundle and with attention to detail, she trimmed the first shingle, positioned it and nailed it into place. She did another, conscious of the boss's scrutiny. "So, how'd I do?" she challenged him.

"All right." He disappeared to the other side of the roof.

She suppressed another giggle and nailed down the next shingle.

Their two hammers pounded a raucous duet— sometimes counterpoint, sometimes in unison. High above Petite, Hannah experienced a freedom and a lightheartedness she hadn't felt for three long years. Her hands busy, her mind wandered. Looking back on it, being engaged to Edward had been similar to a prison sentence, one she'd given herself. She realized that she'd never really "understood" the real Edward. She'd fallen in love with the life they'd have together as pastor and wife.

Today she didn't feel like the same woman who'd worn Edward's speck of a diamond. That struck her as good, but unnerving. If marrying Edward and being a pastor's wife wasn't what she was intended to be, what was? She'd had a plan for her life, but no more. Coping with this fact felt similar to shingling a roof without any safety harness. It was scary, sweaty-palms scary.

Forcing herself to concentrate on the task at hand, she measured and hammered, staggering the notches of the shingles and overlapping them to insure water resistance. She'd hadn't shingled for over a year. Her straining arm and shoulder muscles would ache in the morning. Oh, yeah!

From her lofty vantage point, she had a view of the little village below, the crisscross of streets and patches of green lawn dotted with leafy trees. Over her shoulder, she stole a glance at Guthrie's mother's backyard where Amber, Jenna and Hunter enjoyed the rare sunny day by climbing and swinging on the bright orange A-frame swing set. Squeals and happy shouts floated on the air, making her grin. Oh, to be as carefree as a child again!

A battered silver pickup drove up the street and parked in front of Martha and Lynda's house. Who was dropping by this late in the afternoon?

"Hey!" Guthrie shouted from the opposite side of the roof. "Carpenter's helper, this is the boss. It's time for a break! Hop to it!"

Hannah chuckled. Guthrie must be coming around if he was teasing her. She climbed to the peak and ducked into the steeple.

Inside, propped against a sawhorse, Guthrie held out a candy bar. "Want one?"

She shook her head. Taking a blue bandanna from her pocket, she wiped her moist forehead. "Don't open that candy bar. I've got something better, a casserole left from my food shoot."

"Is it edible?" he teased.

"Watch it, Guthrie! I'm holding a hammer!" She waved it at him, then dropped it into her open tool-box. "Let's go to the kitchen." She jogged down the steps, and he followed her.

In the kitchen, she opened the white refrigerator, took out the green bean casserole and put it in the microwave. While it rotated and warmed, she pulled paper plates and two forks out of the well-stocked kitchen cupboards.

Guthrie lifted two soft drink cans from the vintage refrigerator and popped both tops for them. The bell on the microwave dinged, and she spooned up a healthy portion for Guthrie and did the same for herself.

"Green beans?" Guthrie looked at his plate.

"Try it. You'll like it." She dug into hers and let the tangy cheese and bacon flavors roll over her tongue. "Mmm."

Guthrie forked up a small bite, chewed, then helped himself to some more. "Good."

"Thank you." Hannah nodded.

"How did the show go today? Did the TV people like it?"

She swallowed quickly before laughter conquered her. Picturing the two great-aunts helping her cook, she vibrated with amusement.

"What's so funny?" He stared at her.

She shook her head, then took a deep breath. "Your great-aunts."

"My aunts? What did they do now?"

She sighed, smiling. "I don't want to insult your family, but what is it with your aunts?"

He exhaled loudly, giving expression to exasperation. "They are eccentric. My mom says they've never really grown up. They're over eighty years old and still act like two young girls."

"I know. But why?"

"Well, they were premature twins back in 1919 and were sickly most of their childhood. They didn't go to school because their mother didn't want them picking up any germs. She taught them at home, and that was pretty much their life until their parents died after World War Two.

"Then my grandfather, their brother, took over and worked the farm with his wife. In the fifties, Grandpa bought his sisters their bungalow in town so they wouldn't have to live with my grandparents or my parents, but they'd still be close enough if they needed help."

"So what you're saying is that they have just lived a sheltered and very dependent life in a small town and that's why they seem to exist in a world, a reality of their own?"

Guthrie shrugged. "I guess so. Exactly what did they do during your live cooking demonstration?"

"They came up and helped me."

Guthrie groaned. "Was my mother there?"

"Yes, but what could she do? She had Hunter in her lap."

"How did you handle it?" he asked.

"Oh, I just ad-libbed my way through it, but the

TV reporter and crew looked like they'd just spent time in the twilight zone."

Guthrie swallowed. "It's my fault. The great-aunts were there in the kitchen when you called me last night and heard about the show."

"I invited them, too!" She playfully punched his rock-hard biceps. "Besides, in a town this size, someone would have told them. Don't worry about it. They certainly kept me on my toes, and since I won't be doing any more live TV demos, I don't think we have anything to be worried about."

"Thanks for being so understanding. I wouldn't have wanted them to get their feelings hurt." He smiled at her. A deep, full, irresistible smile.

Funny little squiggly shocks snaked through her arms and legs. Guthrie Thomas smiling at her at close range was obviously too much for her resistance. Fighting his effect on her, she imagined Captain Kirk asking Scotty for the defense shields to be put up. Brushing her unnerving reaction aside, she nonchalantly offered more of the casserole. "Seconds?"

"Please. This is really good. I like the cheese and bacon flavor with the beans."

"You have a discriminating palate, sir." She gave him another generous helping of the creamy white and green casserole. "Why don't you take the rest of this home with you tonight so your family can finish it up? It will just go to waste here."

"Thanks."

"You might be having company tonight for supper."

Guthrie's expression asked a question.

"When I was up on the roof, I saw an older silver-toned truck I didn't recognize pull up to your mother's house."

Guthrie pushed away from the table and hustled toward the hall to the side door.

Hannah stood up. "Guthrie, what's wrong?"

"I'll be back!" Guthrie's farewell was followed by the slamming of the church door.

Whatever did I say to cause that reaction?

Chapter Six

His heart pumping double time, Guthrie bolted out of the church, his anger outracing his feet. When he reached his sister's corner, he caught himself and slowed down. What if this was a false alarm? The person in his sister's house might not be whom he suspected it was at all. But like a waving red flag, the battered pickup sat in plain sight in front of the little yellow house on Church Street.

Taking even breaths, Guthrie walked up the short path and into the house. He paused and closed the door behind him without a sound. If it wasn't the man he dreaded, he'd turn around and go back to the church. Underneath the outside noise of the kids' shouting and squealing, he detected the sound of muted voices in the kitchen. Why were the voices low? That sounded fishy.

He started forward, but his steps slowed—it was like walking up to a ticking package. If the person he thought was in the kitchen actually was in the kitchen, it would upset everything.

In the kitchen doorway, Guthrie stopped.

Mom looked up from where she sat at the table. Her eyes widened.

Guthrie recognized the back of the man's head. The sight sucked the breath right out of him.

The man stood and slowly turned to face him. "Guthrie."

"You." Words roared through Guthrie's head, but only one came out. *"You."*

A ball of fire torched Guthrie's stomach. A red haze clouded his vision. His right fist shot forward.

Billy dodged to the left, then stumbled out of range.

"Guthrie!" his mother exclaimed. "Stop that right now! Beating up your brother-in-law won't help matters."

Gritting his teeth, Guthrie clenched and unclenched his hands. If anyone ever deserved a beating for all he'd done, his sorry excuse for a brother-in-law did!

"Billy has come back to town," Martha said.

"Obviously!" The word burned Guthrie's throat.

Martha went on as though he hadn't spoken. "Billy's cleaned up his life and has come back to shoulder responsibility for his three children."

"They're not his children. They're *our* children. We're raising them with Lynda."

"I truly regret that." Billy spoke in a quiet voice.

Guthrie singed Billy with a glare. "I'm not talking to you. You're not here."

"I am here."

"Not for long." Guthrie was insistent.

"Stop it right now." His mother held up one hand to each man. "Billy left. Billy's back. He's coming again this evening when the kids are in bed to talk to Lynda and see how she wants to handle this."

"How long has he been here?"

The icy words startled Guthrie. He turned to the screen door. Lynda stared in at them. His sister's accusing tone made Guthrie feel guilty—even though he'd done nothing to bring his deadbeat brother-in-law back to Petite.

"How long has he been here?" Lynda repeated coldly.

Billy took a step toward her. "I moved back yesterday. I'm at my mother's. I'd like to talk to you."

Lynda stared him down. "No."

"Mommy!" Hunter called in breathless excitement. "Mommy, look, I'm swinging all by myself!"

Lynda turned. "That's great, Hunter!" She looked at the occupants of the kitchen and said in a frigid tone, "I don't want you upsetting the children. Please leave."

"I'll go for now, Lynda. When you're ready to talk, let me know."

Lynda walked toward her children.

Billy passed Guthrie. He walked out the front door.

Guthrie shivered. Lynda had doused the fire in his gut.

His mother sat, folded her hands in front of her face and wept.

A few minutes later, Guthrie found himself climbing onto the roof from the steeple opening. He'd walked to the church in a daze. Hannah's hammering sounded in his ears and echoed through his body.

Seeing Billy over three years after his desertion, Guthrie felt pounded, battered, and the sound of the hammer intensified this. Suddenly weak in the knees, he sat in the steeple opening. Billy here in town? He couldn't believe it.

"Is that you, Guthrie?" Hannah shouted.

"Yeah," he answered hoarsely.

"You got a call while you were away. Benard's Building Supply called to say they have the zinc strips and the rest of the shingles that were on back order. We can pick them up any time."

The energy had leaked out of Guthrie. He couldn't have raised a hammer if he tried. Going to Benard's would be a good excuse to get away for a while. "Let's go."

"You go. I'll stay and work."

He inhaled. "This is your boss speaking. I won't leave you on this roof alone. Pack up your hammer and nails. You can go home or you can come with me. Your choice."

"All right. I'll come. I want to look at wallpaper and paint. Mom wants me to bring samples back to her."

He heard Hannah's footsteps as she levered herself to the peak of the roof. He was glad she was coming along. Her presence would distract him.

Inside the attic, he undid his worn leather tool belt.

She led him down the attic stair-steps and another flight down to the basement office.

"Mom, I am going to Benard's with Guthrie."

Her mother halted her typing at the word processor. "Thank you, dear. You know the paint colors and wallpaper styles I would be interested in."

Hannah gave her mother a kiss on her forehead. "Love you."

"Love you, too."

Hannah led him out to the truck. He automatically opened the door for her, then he got behind the wheel. Guthrie wondered if his mother was still crying at home.

Something was wrong.

Hannah studied Guthrie from the corner of her eye. In just the few days she'd known this man, she'd come to expect his low-key good humor. Earlier, from her high perch, she'd watched him run to his mother's house and seen Lynda drive up and walk to the back door. Within minutes, a stranger had hurried out the front door and into his truck, then driven away. What did it all mean? The cheerful light in Guthrie's eyes had been snuffed. Why?

"Is your mother all right?" she asked tentatively.

"She's fine."

Next possibility. "You needed something at home?"

"No."

Okay, then. "Your sister came home from work early?"

"Yeah."

Last question. "Your mother had a visitor?"

"That's none of your business!" he exploded.

So the stranger was the problem. She looked out the window on her side. "Sorry."

A few moments passed, then Guthrie said, "I'm sorry. I didn't mean to blow up at you." He sounded miserable and grumpy at the same time.

"No, I'm sorry. I'm afraid I'm so used to having people confide in my parents, and sometimes even in me, that I assume too much. I'll try to remember curiosity killed the cat." She kept her gaze on the scenery, giving him space to grapple with whatever this stranger meant to him.

They'd left Petite far behind them. Lush green cornfields and hayfields, verdant pastures like luxuriant green carpet dotted with black and white Holsteins, Wisconsin's favorite dairy cattle, passed her window.

He cleared his throat. "What kind of wallpaper...I mean, what room is your mother planning to wallpaper?"

Hannah recognized his invitation to smooth things over and go on with the day. She offered him a warm smile. "Mom likes wallpaper or a border in almost every room. She had me bring her samples from several stores in Milwaukee, but she's still looking. She loves to decorate, and she loves looking at samples of wallpaper and paint chips."

"Just like my mother. I remember when she decided to strip the wallpaper off our kitchen walls at the farm. She wanted to paint and hand-stencil a border around the room. She started stripping and ended up taking off nine different layers of wallpaper before she reached the wall itself.''

"Nine? How old is your farmhouse?''

"Built in 1909.''

"Nearly a hundred years old.'' She teased him with a grin. "After your mom took off the wallpaper, did the walls cave in?''

"Very funny. No, but she did have something to say about people who wallpaper over wallpaper over wallpaper.'' He chuckled.

She joined him. The Guthrie she knew was coming back. From the corner of her eye, she watched him drive. Observing this man was pure pleasure. It wasn't just his physical attractiveness. Today his customary peace had been ruffled, but his solid aura of strength and honesty drew her spirit to his. Guthrie Thomas was a man a woman could count on for a direct answer and kindness. Unfortunately, she'd only imagined Edward had those qualities.

She kept up an easy flow of conversation until they parted at the crowded entrance of Benard's. Though still concerned over her new boss's moodiness, she spent several happy minutes picking out wallpaper and border samples and paint chips. The paint manager stood nearby mixing a custom shade of peach for a young red-haired mother who was expecting a child and had a baby boy sitting in her cart, jabbering to passersby.

Hannah waved her pinkie finger at the little guy,

which made him squeal with excitement. She selected a paint chip for that same shade of peach, one of her mother's favorite colors. She also picked up the latest do-it-yourself sheets on rag painting and feather painting. Her creative mother might want to try her hand at those.

Smiling, she met Guthrie at the front entrance. She loved the bustle of customers around them, pushing carts top-heavy with area rugs, light bulbs, plant food, paint and much more.

Carrying the long, narrow, silvery zinc strips that would prevent moss from growing on the roof, he led her to the truck. Then he drove them through the lumber yard entrance and loaded the shingles, which had finally come in. He headed the truck toward Petite.

Only a few miles from home, Hannah saw a welcome sign hand-painted on plywood. Farmers' Market Today! She grabbed Guthrie's arm.

He glanced over at her touch. "What?"

"We have to stop at the farmers' market." Her hand still gripped the bottom of his arm, his warm skin within her grasp.

"But you're not cooking. I mean you're living at the motel." He glanced at her hand.

"I'm sorry." She released his arm, abashed at herself. She went on in a steady voice, suppressing the urge to foolishly apologize for her lingering touch. "That doesn't matter. I can't resist a farmers' market. You never know what you might find!"

"Okay, whatever you say." He pulled the truck into an empty spot in the row of trucks and cars, then

parked in matted wild grass. Nearby a double row of
tables had been set up at the front of a county park
with a ball diamond in the distance. Some vendors
stood behind tables, some sold from the backs of their
pickups. An abundance of sweet corn, zucchini, cabbage, tomatoes and muskmelon in bushel baskets
gave the air a sweet scent.

Hannah jumped out of the truck, avoiding mud
from yesterday's rain. She gazed at the feast of color,
light green, dark green, red-orange and gold. This was
her kind of place.

She stopped to admire the sweet corn in the back
of an old, rusted red pickup.

"Picked fresh today. Do you want one dozen or
two?" the grandmother in blue jeans and a ball cap
asked.

"Just a half dozen. I don't have any place to store
it." She'd fix it for her parents for lunch tomorrow
in the church kitchen.

"Well, if you're feeding Guthrie Thomas, you'll
need half a dozen just for him." The woman chuckled
and winked at Guthrie, standing behind Hannah.

"Thanks for reminding me!" Hannah snapped
open the paper bag the woman had given her and
began choosing a dozen plump ears. She stripped the
outer husk and punctured a kernel to watch the milky
juice spurt out. The white and yellow kernels looked
like rows of exotic pearls.

Guthrie nodded at the woman politely. "This is
Hannah Kirkland, our new pastor's daughter."

"Oh, hi! I thought I recognized you. I saw you on

TV today. Hey, Karen, this is the new pastor's daughter in Petite. You saw her today on the noon show, didn't you?''

For the first time in her career, Hannah found herself mobbed. She definitely wasn't in Milwaukee anymore! Women swarmed around her, each vying for her attention.

''I have your first cookbook. I wish I'd brought it so you could sign it.''

''Your recipes helped me lower my husband's cholesterol twenty-nine points!''

''I thought it was so sweet of you to let the Thomas sisters help you on today's show.''

''Imagine someone letting Ida and Edith cook with them! You must be a saint!''

From across the way, Lila Fink waved to her.

After speaking to everyone, Hannah thanked them and walked over to her landlady. ''Hello, Lila.'' Hannah felt a bit dizzy after so much attention. ''What are you doing here?''

''I'm helping out my sister. She sells fresh eggs and weaves these rugs.''

Hannah looked down. ''These are beautiful rugs.'' Hannah stroked the lush warp and weave of the multishaded white, buff and gray rugs and shook her head. ''Does she make rugs to special order?''

''Sure. Just tell her the size you need.''

''Lady! Lady, do you want a kitty?'' A little dark-haired girl with a pixie haircut held up a little yellow tabby with a fat baby belly.

''Oh! He's precious!'' Hannah took the tiny ball of

silky fur in both hands. The kitten mewled until she
cradled it close to her face. She'd wanted a cat of her
own for years, but Edward hadn't liked cats.

"Do you want them, lady? I got three left, two
from one mama cat and one from another one. Their
eyes are opened, and they're ready to leave their ma-
mas."

"I'm sorry, honey. But I'm living in Mrs. Fink's
motel and I can't have a kitty."

"Sure you can," Lila said. "Cats don't make any
mess."

"You mean it?" Hannah felt as giddy as when she
was a six-year-old and her father had brought home
her first kitten.

"Can you take two more?" the little girl asked
plaintively. "We don't need anymore barn cats at our
place."

Hannah shook her head, then stopped. "Yes, I'll
take one more for my mother." She giggled. "She'll
need a new cat for her new house."

"I'll take the last one." Guthrie spoke up. "Amber
and Jenna have been asking for one."

"Hey, Guthrie," Lila asked abruptly, "what's your
no-account brother-in-law doing back in town?"

Hannah watched Guthrie's tanned face redden. So
that's who'd upset him!

"He won't be around for long." The ugly tone
Guthrie used worried her. It revealed the depth of the
anger and pain he was experiencing. How must Lynda
be suffering? A homecoming should be joyful, not
agonizing.

Guthrie accepted the final cat from the little girl, then asked brusquely, "Hannah, did you need anything else?"

Hannah took the hint in his question. "No, that's all. Lila, please tell your sister my mother will be getting in touch with her about ordering some area rugs."

"Okay." Lila glanced apologetically at the tall man standing beside Hannah. "Sorry if I upset you, Guthrie. It was just such a shock to see Billy in town yesterday."

"No problem," Guthrie said in such a way that reiterated that it was a big problem.

Carrying her two kittens, Hannah walked beside him to the truck. The soft gray kitten looked out of place cradled in the crook of his powerful arm. One of her golden kittens still mewed, but the one in Guthrie's arm looked around, trusting, enjoying the ride. Back in the truck, she took charge of the three kittens.

While Guthrie drove, she sat Indian-style, letting them nest in her lap. Their sharp little claws slipped right through her heavy denim shorts. "Ouch!" she scolded them with a giggle in her throat. Murmuring to them, she stroked under their chins, making them purr and arch their necks, begging for more.

The silent man beside her drew her sympathy. But she knew better than to wound him by saying anything. At this point, even the most kindly meant words might cause pain instead of comfort. *I'm so sorry for you, Guthrie, and your family and for the pain and worry Lynda must be feeling, too! Lord, you know what has gone before and what is happening now. Please be with this family and help the right things happen. Work your miracle of love!*

When he turned into town, Guthrie finally spoke, "I'm sorry. I'm letting my bad mood get me down, and you don't deserve to be ignored like this."

"That's all right. I realized earlier when you took off from the roof so suddenly that something was wrong. Do you want to talk about it?"

He made a sound of disgust. "I just didn't think we'd ever have to deal with him. He took off right after Lynda delivered Hunter prematurely." He paused as though remembering something he didn't want to recall. He shook his head. "It hit everyone hard."

"How awful for your sister, for your family."

"He's done enough damage. I'm not going to let him do any more! Lynda has worked hard to get over the pain and make a life for herself and the kids. I won't let him jeopardize them again."

She touched his arm for the second time that day. "You might not be able to do anything. Since they were legally married, I'm sure he'll be able to get visitation rights, at least." She caught the boldest kitten as it tried to crawl off her lap.

"I'll do something."

She thought he cursed under his breath.

"I'll do something," he repeated.

The Sunday morning sun gilded the tops of the golden oak pews. The small stained glass window high on the wall behind her father glowed with brilliant red, blue and gold. Hannah knew something had upset the people sitting around her, but she couldn't put her finger on the uneasy emotion she sensed.

She sat in the second pew, next to her mother, as she always had in church, and watched her father lead the first Sunday service she'd attended in Petite. The service had begun normally with a prelude and greeting, then a hymn. During the singing of "Bringing in the Sheaves," a disturbed rustle had gone through the congregation.

Hannah had glanced over her shoulder and observed a young man in clean but worn clothing take his seat in a back pew. Her head wasn't the only one that had turned. The rustle was from the craning of necks and heated whispers.

The arrival of the stranger seemed to paralyze the congregation. Everyone, even the children, stilled. Was this man's presence the cause of the tension around her? If Hannah had brought a thermometer into the sanctuary, she knew the temperature in the room would read chilling. Was this Guthrie's brother-in-law?

If she could have glimpsed the Thomas family's reaction she would have had her answer. But they sat several rows behind her, and she couldn't see them unless she stood up and turned completely around. And, of course, she couldn't do that.

Maybe this wasn't Lynda's ex at all. He could be some other member in a small-town feud who'd entered enemy territory.

This was one of the factors that made switching congregations perilous for a new pastor. No matter what the Bible said about loving one another and forgiving, most churches had some person who acted as a lightning rod. Someone who sparked controversy her parents would have to neutralize, or there would be unpleasant conflict within the church.

Hannah bowed her head. *Dear Lord, whatever this man has done or left undone, please don't let this little church fall into conflict. It's so sad, Lord, to see people who should know the most about loving and forgiving begin to squabble and separate themselves from each other. Oh, Lord, please bind up the spirit of discord and take it far from us here. Bless my father and mother, give them the right words to say and the right actions to take. Amen.*

Hannah felt better immediately. She'd done right this time, not stewing, but turning everything straight over to God.

She glanced up. Her father was smiling at her. She smiled back. The service continued. All through the sermon, the stiff uneasiness in the congregation went unabated. Finally, the organ played the closing hymn, "Just As I Am."

Praying for peace with each word, Hannah sang, "Without one plea, but that your blood was shed for me."

Her father stepped forward to give the benediction.

As if on cue, the stranger walked forward down the center aisle runner of worn maroon carpeting and up the two steps to the pulpit. "If you don't mind, pastor, I'd like to say a few words."

A rustle of startled murmurs passed through the congregation.

Hannah held her breath. Would her questions be answered now?

Her father looked surprised, but asked, "What kind of words?"

"An apology."

Hannah stared at the man. *Oh, my, an apology given from a pulpit. That is very rare. Dad, help him.*

Her father nodded and motioned everyone to sit down, then stepped away.

The young man stood beside the wood pulpit with one trembling hand resting on it and looked out over the congregation. "You all know me, except for your new pastor. You know what I've done and that I ran away. I guess you could call me Petite's prodigal son. I've spent the past three years in Chicago living on the streets. Drugs took me there, put me there, kept me there." The man wiped sweat from his forehead.

The congregation sat in total silence, even the children.

Hannah ached for him. He stood alone. The story of the prodigal son played in her mind. The prodigal had said, "Father, I have sinned against God and against you. I am not fit to be called your son."

"About a year ago in Chicago, I staggered into the Salvation Army near Maxwell Street looking for a meal and a bed for the night. I got more than that. That night for the first time I faced up to what my addiction had done to me, to my family. That night I promised God I'd get off drugs if He would stand with me. Since you know God, you all know what His answer was.'' The man stood a little straighter.

The deep emotion in his plain words touched Hannah. She blinked away tears.

''I've been clean since that night. I went through a substance abuse program, and I attend AA meetings weekly. I know most of you never wanted to see my face again, but once I came back to my right mind, I knew I had to come back home. I have responsibilities. I have a job in Portage and will be staying with my mother and assuming responsibility for the family I left behind. I hope you will all give me a second chance. But I won't blame you if you don't.'' The man stepped down and walked to the back of the church.

Hannah glanced around. She wasn't the only one grappling with overwhelming emotion. Everyone looked stunned. She could only think of Guthrie's sister. This man must be Billy.

At the end of the benediction, Dad said the final amen and everyone stood up. Hannah noticed that, as one, they refused to look at the stranger. She'd heard the Amish used shunning on members who didn't conform. Evidently this congregation was so shocked they couldn't confront the man. Instead, everyone gathered around Lynda and her family as though trying to protect them. Lynda's face looked frozen, pained.

As Hannah had expected, however, her father made

a beeline to the stranger, shook his hand and talked to him for several minutes while everyone else pointedly kept their attention elsewhere. Wasn't anyone going to speak to him? Finally, the stranger walked out of the sanctuary.

Hannah watched him go. *Dear Lord, you've sent Mom and Dad a tough one this time.*

Chapter Seven

The shrill ring of the phone by the bed woke Hannah. In the midnight darkness, she groped for the receiver while trying to bring the bedside clock face, the only circle of light in the room, into focus. "Hello?"

"Gotcha!" Doree's voice giggled in her ear.

"Oh, go to bed." Hannah closed her eyes. "It's after one a.m. Why aren't you asleep?"

"I'm back on campus. Who goes to sleep before two a.m. around here?"

"Do I care? Good—"

"No! Tell me how Mom and Dad are and how the search is going."

"Haven't you talked to Spring?"

"No. I'm talking to you."

Hannah came fully awake. No use trying to go back to sleep. She sat up in bed, arranging her feather pillow behind her, then leaning against it. Fatigue made her whole body feel heavier than normal. Lifting her arm compared to lifting a twenty-pound bag of cement.

"Doree, I thought you'd stop here on your way back to Madison."

"Couldn't. My car died for the last time in Milwaukee and I had to hitch a ride with a few friends. I couldn't ask them to stop. What's up? What was Spring going to tell me?"

Hannah sighed. Doree wouldn't like the answer. "Mom and Dad's house isn't going to be ready on time." The little golden kitten Hannah had adopted woke up from where it slept near her side. It baby-mewed softly as it yawned.

"Oh? How far is it from being finished?"

"They have a foundation." The stark image of her parents' forlorn foundation came to Hannah's mind.

"And?"

"And nothing else." The issue, the unfinished house, had been overshadowed in Hannah's mind by the dramatic return of Lynda's ex. What did wood and cement matter when human hearts remained broken? The worrying thoughts Hannah had finally eluded with sleep rushed back, seizing her dog-tired mind.

Last Sunday evening, Dad had talked to Mom and Hannah about Billy and Lynda, then they had prayed for healing and reconciliation. So far their prayers hadn't moved Lynda. Nearly a week had passed and still she hadn't spoken to Billy. The town of Petite watched, frowned and murmured. Several had called her father, though Dad couldn't force Lynda to deal with the issue. Last night, Martha had called Dad and asked him to speak to Lynda. So he had walked over after the children had gone to bed. No luck. She'd politely thanked him for his concern and turned away. But ignoring Billy wouldn't make him go away.

Doree's voice broke in on Hannah's thoughts. "Hey, you're not listening to me. I said, and I quote, 'A foundation, just a foundation! Is this some kind of sick joke?' And are you trying to get out of looking for Mom's adoption papers?"

Hannah's emotions felt worn thin, like the 1970s faded harvest gold sheets on her bed. "Doree, the rain has delayed the house."

"Hey, it hasn't rained that much since June."

"Dad's church's roof needed to be replaced by the same builder." The kitten climbed onto Hannah's lap.

"And, of course, our parents said, 'No problem. We'll wait.' Sheesh!"

"Yes, you've got the picture." Hannah worried her lower lip.

"Darn." Rock music screeched in the background in Doree's dorm. "You can't do a thing about the adoption papers until the house is done. Everything's in storage."

"Too true."

"You're not trying to weasel out then?"

"Weasel out? In Milwaukee, I told you I'd think about it." Hannah's kitten kneaded her gold twill bedspread with its tiny paws, then curled up to go back to sleep, purring.

"So? Did you *think* about it?"

Yes, in between helping Guthrie, writing her column and outlining her next cookbook, she had pondered and prayed about searching for her mother's biological family. She wished she could wipe her mind clean of prodigal fathers, inclement weather and her mother's leukemia. "Quite a bit."

"And?"

"I'm beginning to think you're right." In fact, Hannah had worried before coming to Petite that she might not have a choice.

"I know I'm right."

"Of course, you do, Doree. You always think you're right!"

Doree ignored her. "Oh, I almost forgot! I saw you on TV! I was in the Student Union eating lunch when I looked up at the wall TV and there you were. Hannah, how did you get on TV?"

Hannah wondered at her sister's flightiness. Straight from discussing their mother's illness to the TV show? "My agent had called them several times in the past trying to get a spot when each of my cookbooks came out, but no luck. Then they called her out of the blue. She gave them my number, and they asked me to fill in their local spot on the noon news. I said yes." Hannah yawned.

"Where were you cooking? I thought, 'If that's Mom's new kitchen, I'm going to strangle the builder even if he is a hunk.' How is he, anyway?"

Doree, let me go back to sleep, please. I don't want

to deal with this now. "I was cooking in the church kitchen, and Guthrie is fine."

"*Guthrie* is fine," Doree's voice teased. "My, we're getting friendly with the builder, aren't we?"

"It's a small town." Hannah recalled the day of the live cooking demonstration, and later, Guthrie's preoccupation on their trip to Portage. He must have known then that his ex-brother-in-law was in town.

Hannah pulled her mind back to the conversation at hand. "Besides, I've begun pitching in to help him get the church done so he can get on with our parents' house."

Doree laughed. "Outrageous! I wish I could see you up on the roof with him."

"Yes, yes, anything else?" Hannah asked wearily. "I have to be up and ready at six for breakfast and at the church by seven."

"Oh, yeah, who were those funny old ladies who were on the show with you? I don't remember seeing them on that station before."

Hannah felt uncomfortable with her sister's careless words. Ida and Edith were sweet, just a little vague on facts and if, because of them, she didn't get asked back to that noon show, the world wouldn't end. "Those were Guthrie's maiden great-aunts who live here in town."

"Don't get huffy. They were great! They were hilarious! Kind of like having an old radio comedy team cooking with you."

One corner of Hannah's mouth crinkled up. "It was funny. Afterwards," she admitted. "During the show when they popped up from the audience, I nearly passed out.''

''You mean you didn't plan on them helping? What a hoot!''

''Yes, and on that note, good night, little baby sister.'' Hannah hung up on a protesting Doree. She said to the receiver, back in its place, '' 'Little baby sister' serves you right for waking me up in the middle of the night.''

With one last pat for her cat, she slid down, glanced at the clock and groaned. Closing her eyes, she tried to relax, tried to empty her mind of all the thoughts she'd been fighting before she finally fell asleep the first time.

Oh, Lord, let your love flow through Petite and change the hearts here. So much pain, so much of the past to be forgiven. Would Lynda give Billy a second chance? Would Guthrie? Did they have a choice?

At six-twenty the next morning, yawning, Hannah walked into Hanson's Cozy Café.

''None of that allowed in here!'' Lila called from behind the worn, speckled Formica counter. ''You'll have us all yawning. Coffee?''

Nodding, Hannah swallowed another yawn, sat down at the counter and placed her order.

Lila called the order to the cook behind her. ''So when do you think Lynda will break down and talk to Billy?''

Shrugging, Hannah tried to think of a polite, non-gossipy reply, but drew a blank. Fortunately or unfortunately, Lila didn't seem to need one.

"Well, I feel sorry for his mother, Terri Sue. She not only lost her son when Billy took off, but she hasn't been able to face Lynda. But he's her only son, and those three children are her only grandchildren."

This bit of news stirred Hannah's sympathy. "I haven't met Terri Sue."

"Well, she isn't very sociable since the trouble with her son. She lives about five miles west of town, works in Portage."

"I'm sorry to hear that. I didn't think Lynda would—"

"Oh, Lynda didn't say Terri Sue couldn't see the children. But the way Billy left and all that happened because he left made his mother too ashamed. Martha even called her after the funeral and told her they didn't bear her any grudge. Real Christian of Martha, I say. It was her husband, after all."

Funeral? Martha's husband? Hannah couldn't follow what Lila was saying, but before she could ask, four boisterous truckers came in demanding breakfast. Lila left the counter to take their orders. Soon she placed Hannah's breakfast in front of her, but was too busy to stop and finish their conversation.

Hannah chewed her buttery eggs and crisp bacon and pondered what Billy could have done that had made his mother so ashamed she couldn't face her grandchildren. Terri Sue was another victim in this family tragedy. Would Hannah ever get used to the way families hurt one another? Spring, Doree and she had been so lucky in the family they'd been born into.

But what about their mother? When…*if* Hannah located the adoption papers, would they lead her and her sisters to another sad, painful story? Giving a child up for adoption must have been the result of one. She bet Doree hadn't thought about that. Hannah closed her eyes and pushed this out of her mind. A heart could only carry so much at one time. She forced herself to finish breakfast and waved goodbye to Lila. On the way out of the restaurant, she stopped at a table to chat with Becky, one of the beauticians at the Bizzy Bee whom she'd met at church. She made an appointment with Becky for a trim and left with a wave. Then she headed to the church for a day on the roof.

By the time the sun had climbed high, Hannah had shingled halfway up her side of the dark green roof. She did know how to shingle a roof, but that didn't mean she was fast. She'd only done it a few times before, but she felt she was getting better, more efficient.

Guthrie, on the other side, sounded close to the peak by the timbre of his hammer. It wasn't like they were competing, but Hannah still didn't like it that she was losing.

"I'll be able to come over and help you after I finish three more rows," Guthrie called as if he'd been reading her mind. "In fact, it's time for a break. Meet me in the steeple."

"Good." She pounded one more roofing nail in.

"I've been thinking," Guthrie shouted.

"Wow! What brought that on?" she teased. She'd tried to act as naturally as possible toward Guthrie since church on Sunday. She surmised he must be suffering internal turmoil, but she couldn't do anything to change what had happened years ago or this week. He'd spent most of the week on his dairy feeder cattle farm, harvesting this winter's hay crop while the fields had been blessedly dry.

The time apart had made it awkward to be working alone with him. She'd hoped he would stop by the motel or church office and open up to her father. Didn't Guthrie realize the danger in which his sister's children stood? It made Hannah feel a little sick every time she imagined Amber, Jenna or little Hunter overhearing something they weren't supposed to hear.

Guthrie didn't reply to her teasing question until he appeared at the peak and looked down at her. The sunshine gilded his tanned arms. Hannah swallowed, trying to moisten her suddenly dry mouth.

He settled his hand on his tool belt. "Very funny. I think I've thought of a way to hurry up your parents' house."

"You what!" Energized, she began pulling herself up to meet him.

He repeated his sentence as she climbed.

"Don't keep me in suspense! What's the idea?"

"Well, you know how I suggested to your parents that they go with a factory-built house?"

"Yes?" She reached the peak.

His hands under her arms, Guthrie swung her effortlessly up the last foot onto the peak, then motioned her to precede him into the steeple opening. She ducked inside.

He thumped down after her. "There's another option I hadn't mentioned to them. Instead of doing the stick-built house that I planned for them, I can order a factory shell."

"What's that?" Tugging off her grimy white cotton gloves, she turned to face him. "They didn't want a factory-built house. How is this different?"

"A shell is the outer walls with windows and doors and roof all manufactured and assembled at the factory. They truck the completed walls here and put them up with a crane. The whole exterior can be put together and enclosed in twelve hours. What do you think of that?"

Words failed Hannah. Twelve hours and the house would be up! She couldn't believe it. She couldn't help herself. She threw her arms around his neck and kissed him.

Guthrie's lips parted with surprise. So close to him, she lost herself in the mingled scents of wood, leather, fresh hay and honest perspiration. Her lips tingled, and she shivered. Sensations, warm and exciting, rippled through her. Needing something solid to hold on to, she tightened her hold around his neck. *Oh, my, this is wonderful. I never knew.... Oh, my...*

Then a quicksilver thought flashed her back to reality. *Oh, no, I'm kissing Guthrie Thomas! What must he think of me?* Before she embarrassed herself more, she pulled away.

"That's a wonderful idea! Twelve hours! Do you mean that? My parents will be ecstatic." Words fell out of her mouth as she tried to distract him from the fact that she'd just kissed him.

Ignoring her words, Guthrie tucked her close again, leaned down and kissed her.

His lips immobilized her. *He kissed me back. What's going on?* She couldn't draw breath. "Guthrie," she finally cautioned, quivering.

A shocked expression on his face, he stepped back. "Sorry. Don't know what got into me."

Her face blazed. *And I don't know what got into me! And Edward never kissed me like that! I never knew....* "My fault. I kissed you first. I was just so excited...."

Guthrie pushed his hands through his moist hair. "It's all this about Lynda's... I don't feel like myself. I would never—"

Hannah touched his forearm. Her glance spoke her sympathy. She wanted to say, "Don't let Lynda wait too long. Someone else might tell the children that their father has come back to town. Lynda should be the one." But she couldn't speak. The look in his blue eyes warned her away.

Changing the subject without saying a word, he glanced over her shoulder toward the stairs. "Let's go down and see what your parents think about my idea."

"Great. Let's go." She automatically tugged off her tool belt and led him down to the church office. The shell could be up in twelve hours. Feeling the first ray of hope in days, she nearly skipped into the office. "Mom, is Dad busy?"

Hannah bent and picked up her kitten from the laundry basket where it snoozed on a frayed white bath towel. Her mom's new cat looked up, blinking sleepily. The little yellow tabby purred in Hannah's ear, then licked her with its tiny sandpaper tongue.

Her mother looked up quizzically and turned to tap on the door behind her. "Garner, can you put your sermon aside for a minute? Hannah and Guthrie want to talk to us."

Dad came out right away. "What about?"

"Guthrie has come up with a great idea," Hannah started, "for speeding up the work on your house."

Immediately her father looked skeptical.

So Hannah stepped aside, motioning toward Guthrie.

Guthrie stood, his weight on his heels. "You know how bad I feel about not being able to get your house done on time? Well, I was thinking the other night that I hadn't told you about a third way to build a house."

"A third way?" Garner asked. "This won't mean a loss of quality?"

"No. You see, it's only the shell." Guthrie rounded his hands together, demonstrating the idea. "I mean, we just order the shell, and it's made at the factory. They truck it in and put it up with a crane—"

"In twelve hours!" Hannah had to interrupt.

Her mother motioned Guthrie to sit down. "Start at the beginning, Guthrie, not the end."

Hannah sat down on the floor to play with the kittens.

Easing into the chair in front of the desk, Guthrie took his time and explained how he'd take the plans to a company in Prairie du Chein and order the custom-made shell, what it would cost and how much time it would save him. "You see, my custom work actually goes into the interior. As it is, I've held off putting down the subfloor for fear of rain damage.

"This way the house would all be enclosed in one day, really. Then I can spend the fall—after haying is done—just working on putting up wallboard, laying flooring and doing the custom work you want done."

"And I'd still help him with that." Hannah grinned so wide it hurt the corners of her jaw. The two kittens with sharp little claws crawled around in her lap, tumbling over each other. Hannah winced as each tiny claw poked her.

"But won't that take away part of your profit?" Dad asked.

"Some. But I figure I'll get yours up and done, and I'll still have time to take on another house and do the same with it, then spend the winter finishing its interior—after yours is done."

"Well, we'll need to talk this over." Her father glanced at her mother.

"Ouchy," Hannah murmured to the kittens. She lifted one in each hand, high above her lap. "I've got to trim your claws, you little sweeties." She set them on the rug.

Her mother nodded. The church phone rang. She

answered it, "Petite Community Church, Ethel speaking."

Hannah looked at Guthrie. "I'm thirsty. I've got sun tea ready for us in the refrigerator."

He smiled, something he hadn't done much since Sunday. "There are some advantages to having you as my carpenter's helper."

Her mother said, "She'll be right over." She hung up. "Hannah, that was the vet. She's had a cancellation this afternoon, and if you go right over, she has time to give the kittens their distemper shots."

Catching her kitten, Hannah rose. "Guthrie, I promised Amber that I'd take her along with her kitty, too. I won't be gone long."

"Okay. I'll drink a glass of sun tea and then go back up on the roof." He bent and scooped up her mother's kitten from beside his work boot. The little ball of gray fur looked minuscule in his large capable hand. "Does Lynda know about this?"

"Yes." Hannah accepted the kitten from him. "Mom, call Martha and tell her I'll be picking up Amber and kitty. That will give them a few minutes to round up the cat."

Within ten minutes, she sat beside Amber in her red SUV. Amber held her velvety gray kitten close to her face. "She's so soft."

"I know." Hannah smiled. "What did you name her?"

"I decided to name her Misty because her fur is like the sky when it's misty outside."

"Amber, what a great name!" Hannah praised the

child and meant it. "And it's given me the perfect name for mine."

"Really? What are you going to call her?" Amber asked.

"Sunny! Because she's golden like a sunny day!"

"Cool," Amber said. "Misty and Sunny. What did your mama name her cat?"

"She hasn't named him yet. She likes to take her time in picking out a name. So we'll just call him Cat until he has an official name."

"Okay."

From one of the county roads, Hannah turned into the graveled parking lot of the vet. Inside the office, barking and meowing sounded from the back where the hospital part was located. Amber and Hannah sat down on a bench in the designated cat side of the waiting room.

The door to the examining rooms opened, and a young female vet in a white lab coat walked out, followed by a man carrying a Chihuahua. Hannah was paying only scant attention to the vet as she talked to the man about bringing the Chihuahua back for a re-examination.

But Amber popped up, walked over and stared at him. When Hannah recognized who the man was, she froze.

Amber announced, "Damon Kinney says you're my daddy."

Chapter Eight

Oh, no! Hannah's worst fear for Lynda's children was happening to Amber right in front of her eyes. Damon Kinney had seen Billy at church just as Amber had, and evidently Damon's parents had discussed who Billy was in front of Damon. Hannah stared at the child and her father, frantically trying to think what to say to defuse the situation, how to protect the little girl's feelings.

"Yes, I am your daddy," Billy said quietly.

"How come you went away and left us?" Amber asked. "You didn't even come back for Christmas."

Hannah wept inside. *Oh, Amber, I'm so sorry. I wanted to prevent this from happening to you, but I couldn't.*

"I was stupid." Billy gazed into his daughter's eyes. "I didn't know then how lucky I was to have your mom and you kids."

"Does that mean you want us back now?" Amber asked with bright hope in every syllable.

Hannah flinched at the vulnerability of this innocent child. She slid forward on the bench to go to Amber, to rescue her.

"It means I know now that you kids and your mom are priceless gifts from God. And I would like to get to know you and your sister and brother." Billy's voice quivered with emotion.

Hannah held her breath.

"Okay." Amber nodded. "You can. We'd like to get to know you. We want to have a daddy."

Amber's simple words pierced Hannah's heart like needles. How freely Amber forgave the father who'd abandoned her. Oh, for the faith of a child!

Billy handed the Chihuahua to the vet and squatted in front of Amber at eye level. "I think you'll have to talk that over with your mother first, Amber. I'm the one who left. Your mother stayed and took care of you kids, so she has to be the one to decide when I can see you. That's why I haven't come to your house to see the three of you yet." He reached out and touched the kitten in Amber's arms. His hand trembled. "Is this your kitty?"

Amber nodded.

The vet looked at Hannah as if to ask what was going on. Hannah shrugged.

The tiny dog in the vet's arms yipped as though reminding Billy of its existence. Billy rose and retrieved the Chihuahua from the vet. "It was nice seeing you, Amber, and I hope to see you again soon."

Hannah wondered what it felt like to have your child treat you like a stranger.

"Okay. I'll ask Mommy."

"You do that." With a drawn expression, Billy nodded to Hannah and walked out.

Amber came back to her. "That was my daddy."

"I heard him." Hannah yearned to hug Amber close, but she didn't want to add any emotion to this already heart-rending incident. Better for the child if Hannah acted as naturally as possible.

"Why didn't Mommy tell me he came back? Damon Kinney knew."

Hannah had also dreaded this inevitable question. How did children unerringly go straight to the heart of the matter? She thought quickly and came up with a careful answer. "Your daddy told you why. It's up to your mother to decide when you would meet your father again."

"Well, I met him."

"Then you'll have to tell your mother that." Not wishing to be asked any more questions, Hannah stood up. Cradling two squirming kittens in one arm, she took Amber's hand and led her to the vet. "Now let's get our three kittens their shots."

What will Guthrie do when I tell him about this? Oh, Lord, deal with Guthrie and Lynda's wounded hearts.

Back in front of the little yellow house on Church Street, Amber waved goodbye to Hannah, then ran up the short path to her house.

Though weighed down with worry, Hannah smiled

and waved back. Then she drove her red SUV back to the church and parked in the gravel lot there. Climbing out of the truck, she was greeted by the rhythmic sound of Guthrie's hammer above her. Without enthusiasm, she walked back into the church and deposited the gray-striped and golden kittens in the blue laundry basket. They immediately pounced on one another, rolling over and over each other.

The office was deserted. Neither her father or mother were in sight. Maybe they'd gone to the kitchen for a coffee break. She considered trying to find them.

But that was cowardly. The man pounding nails on the roof was the one she needed to talk to. Her father had already tried to make Lynda see reality. Maybe it was time for her to shake Guthrie up. *God, as Paul stood up to Peter, give me the strength to stand up to Guthrie Thomas and move him to talk his sister into dealing with this crisis. Stand by my side and give me the strength of Samson and the wisdom of Solomon. I'll need both.*

With this prayer in her heavy heart, she mounted the stairs, pulled on her tool belt and crawled through the steeple opening. "Guthrie, I'm back!"

"I thought you'd decided to take the rest of the day off. How long does it take to get three kittens vaccinated?" Guthrie had finished his side and had started on hers. About one-quarter remained undone.

His unconcerned tone deepened her regret at having to bring bad tidings. "It took as long as it needed." After slipping on her work gloves, she hooked her safety harness and let herself down the side of the roof. Just over two weeks ago, getting her parents' house done on time had been the big issue in her mind. Now it paled in comparison to this family's crisis. She settled at the other end of the roof from Guthrie.

He finished pounding a nail. "I think we can get this done if we stay at it the rest of the afternoon."

Hannah tried to think of a gentle way to tell him what had happened at the vet's. No easy way presented itself.

She lifted the hammer from her belt, reached for a shingle, then a nail. She clung to her resolve. God had let Amber meet her father in front of Hannah. He'd dropped the hot potato in *her* lap. She couldn't let Amber down.

"Guthrie, we're going to have to talk about..." Pausing, she positioned the shingle and began pounding it in, one stroke for each word. "Some... thing...you...don't...want...to...talk...about."

"I'm not talking about Billy." He continued hammering.

She ignored his stubbornness. "Today when Amber and I were at the vet, the thing I dreaded the most for your niece happened right in front of me."

"What did he do!" Guthrie roared. "Did he follow you there?"

Where had her gentle carpenter gone, the man who could laugh about being startled off a roof? "He didn't follow us. He was already there."

Guthrie charged ahead. "Did he get that new vet to call you?"

"Guthrie, stop frothing at the mouth and let me tell you what happened!"

He replied by viciously pounding a nail into place.

Hannah's temper frayed. "You need to listen to me!" She shook her hammer at him. "You don't even know what happened yet."

He glared at her, but closed his lips as if his mouth was stuffed with one-penny nails.

"I didn't notice him at first, but…" She paused for effect and waited for him to let her know he was listening.

After a moment, he said, "But? Go on!"

She took a deep breath, bracing herself. "But Amber noticed him. She walked up to him."

"What? You let her talk to him!"

"I was in shock! I couldn't move. It was like watching a dream, a nightmare. She walked up to him and said, 'Damon Kinney says you're my daddy.'" Hannah turned to Guthrie.

He wouldn't meet her gaze, but stared at the shingles beneath his boots. His anger appeared to have deserted him. "Why would the Kinneys tell their boy about Billy? I don't get it."

Oh, Guthrie, are you being dense on purpose? "Didn't you realize some husband and wife here would talk about Billy and that their children might overhear it and repeat it to Lynda's children? I've been dreading this since Sunday." She positioned another shingle and banged in the first nail.

Guthrie remained silent.

Hannah went on pounding in nails. When the shingle was done, she turned to him. His expression shocked her. "Guthrie!"

His face was twisted with pain.

Seeing his anguish, she wondered if Billy had done more than abandon Lynda. Lila's mention of Guthrie's dad and his funeral came back to her. Billy had done more than desert his family, hadn't he?

Guthrie answered her unspoken question. "You don't know all he did." Emotion clogged his throat.

"What did he do?" Hannah slung her hammer in her belt. Still tethered by the harness, she jumped sideways to him. "Tell me. Please."

He looked away, obviously fighting not to break down. He mastered himself. "Lynda was pregnant with her third, with Hunter. She started to go into premature labor. Billy was out somewhere, doing who knows what."

He turned to her as though appealing for her understanding. "Lynda called me. I drove her to the hospital in Portage. She delivered the baby nearly six weeks early. He was in neonatal intensive care." Guthrie took a deep breath. "We didn't know if he...if Hunter would live, if he would suffer brain damage."

Hannah ached inside for Lynda and her family. "Did Billy finally come?"

"Yes, his mother found him and dragged him to the hospital. He took one look at Hunter, hooked up to all kinds of tubes, and ran out of the hospital."

Hannah didn't know what to say, but she had a feeling she knew what happened next. "He left town then?"

"Yeah, but first he knocked down his own mother when she tried to stop him, took every penny out of Lynda's and his savings account. He took the money Lynda had earned waitressing at Lila's to pay for the delivery. They didn't have insurance. The costs for Hunter's care were astronomical. The hospital forgave some, but I had to take out a second mortgage on our farm in order to pay them."

Guthrie kicked the roof below his right foot. "Now he's back, maybe he's figured how to get money out of Lynda, probably by holding the kids over her. And I won't let that druggy deadbeat around Lynda's children."

Feeling dragged down by his story of pain, Hannah couldn't argue with the cause of his distrust of Billy, but that didn't matter now. That was then, this was now. But she sensed he was holding something back. Right now their plate was full. "You don't want Billy around his children, but you don't have a choice."

"Yes, I do!" He glared at her.

She gripped his shoulder. Through the cotton of his blue T-shirt she felt his strength, his resistance. "Amber wants to know her father. No matter what he's done, a child wants to know, and if possible, to be loved by her father."

"He's just come back to do it to us all over again! He hasn't changed! He's got some scam up his sleeve."

"Even if you're right, it doesn't change what I've just said. Amber knows. Do you hear me?" She moved her face within inches of his. His warm, sweet breath wafted over her face. She remembered the kisses they'd shared that morning. Hard to believe so much could happen in one day. Guthrie drew her, an honest man who was easy to like.

The temptation to touch his cheek, to soothe his pain rocked her. She tried to ignore it. They were still nearly strangers. "If Amber has found out about her father, you know she's told Jenna and Hunter. They'll want to see their father. It's only natural."

"No."

"Do you know what Amber said to Billy? She said, 'We want a daddy.'" She stopped to let this sink in, then she said more kindly, "You've got to talk to Lynda before she gets home tonight, so she will be prepared. How she handles this with the children is crucial. If you're right, Lynda needs to be the rock her children cling to. She has to show them they can count on her. You understand that, don't you?"

"What exactly did he say to Amber?" Guthrie asked in a gruff voice.

Hannah rejoiced at this. He'd finally begun to listen to her and face the immediate problem. "He said that since he was the one who left, Lynda would have to decide when he could see the children."

"I hate this!" Guthrie spat out the words. "Why did God let him come back here?"

Hannah shook her head. *Do I know the mind of God?* "You can hate Billy's return, but you have to take action or things could get worse, much worse for the children.''

He stared at her, looking drained of his usual energy.

''The children and their feelings are what are important today. Billy hurt all of you deeply over three years ago. But your pain isn't the focus now. Amber, Jenna and Hunter have already had to deal with being deserted by their father. They shouldn't have to witness their mother fall apart in front of their eyes when their father returns.''

Glancing away, he wiped his forehead with a pocket bandanna.

''On Sunday, Billy said he was the prodigal son. Remember in that parable, the older brother wasn't happy to see his baby brother back, either. But the father said, 'Your brother who was dead is now alive. I must rejoice.' If Billy has truly changed—''

''He hasn't.''

Impatient, Hannah ordered, ''Go.''

''What?''

She didn't waste any words. ''Go to the parking lot at Lynda's job and wait for her to come out. You have to talk to her, tell her what's happened.''

''What will I say?''

His plea touched her. ''Just tell her everything. If she still can't deal with seeing Billy with the children, bring her back here. My dad and mom will do everything they can to help her.'' She shoved his shoulder, urging him up the roof. ''Go. I'll keep at this. Go.''

Guthrie grimaced, but pulled himself up to the peak and disappeared into the steeple. Within minutes, she heard his blue truck screech out of the church parking lot.

She reached for another shingle. It was good to have something to do. Hammering nails let her release the anger she felt at this wicked world where innocent children suffered for the sins of their parents. "God go with you, Guthrie," she murmured.

Hannah had just started the final row of dark green shingles when she glimpsed Guthrie's truck pull into the parking lot. Lynda's modest beige sedan trailed right behind. Hannah kept working on the roof, but prayed with each stroke of her hammer that God ould begin healing this broken family.

Soon, Guthrie ducked out of the steeple, hooked his harness on and let himself down right beside her. "You've got a lot done."

"I pray good with a hammer in my hand." She gave him a tiny smile, just a quirking up of the corners of her mouth. "Or I hammer good while I pray."

"Lynda's talking to your dad now." He sounded detached.

Though longing to hold this tenderhearted man close and comfort him, Hannah merely nodded. "I'm glad you went and spoke to her."

He picked up a shingle and positioned it. "I didn't have a choice."

Hannah recalled the kisses they'd shared, the sensation of his lips on hers. Pushing these dangerous thoughts out of her mind, she concentrated on the work at hand.

They didn't talk any further, but finished the final row together, then hoisted themselves up and into the church. Hannah ran her fingers through her moist hair.

"I wish I could enjoy this moment more. I thought I'd never get this roof done," Guthrie said. He touched her shoulder. "Thanks, you really helped. But you can retire now. The church is done."

She gave him what she hoped was one of those enigmatic smiles she'd read about. "We'll see. My parents haven't agreed to the factory-built shell. You may not know it, but you need me, Guthrie Thomas."

A voice came from below. "Hannah! Hannah!"

Hannah stepped to the top of the stairs. "Mother?"

"Come down! There's a phone call for you! Your father and I are going to take Lynda home now to talk to the children."

"Okay, Mom!" Hannah turned to Guthrie. "That's peculiar. Who would be calling me here?" She undid her tool belt and draped it on the sawhorse. "I'll be back to help you pack up stuff."

"That's all right. I'm exhausted, but I don't know why. You finished the job. I'll just close up the steeple. I'll start tomorrow shutting down this job."

Nodding, Hannah skipped down the steps. At her mother's desk, she picked up the phone and leaned against the desk. "Hello, this is Hannah Kirkland speaking."

* * *

Guthrie trailed after Hannah. The day had sapped his strength, his joy of accomplishment. He would have done anything to spare Lynda this grief. Wrecking things seemed to be Billy's specialty. Lynda was finally on her feet, and the pain from the past had faded. So, of course, Billy came to stir everything up again.

At Hunter's birth, Billy had carved a deep wound into all their hearts. His coming back to town had ripped the scab off. Guthrie wanted to kick him into next week. He struggled with the anger that spurted inside him every time he pictured Billy's face. What had little Amber thought of her father today? How would this affect the children? They deserved better than Billy.

"Oh? Really?" Hannah's voice sounded loud in the quiet office. The kittens in their basket were mewing for her attention and trying to climb out to reach her.

Guthrie glanced at Hannah, then did a double-take. She had the strangest expression on her face. Who was she talking to on the phone?

"I see. That's very interesting," Hannah commented in an odd tone.

Guthrie bent and picked up both kittens from the white terry-cloth towel in the basket. He cradled them on one arm, stroking their tiny heads and listening to their little engines purring.

"I think that will work. You'll let me know the details of the agreement? Very well. Thank you for calling. This is good news. Goodbye.'' Hannah hung up the phone.

Guthrie waited for her to explain who she'd been talking to. Finally, he prompted, ''Well?''

Hannah stared at him. She looked like she'd swallowed something too big for her.

''Did something bad happen?''

''No, I just...this is so funny...you'll never believe it.'' Hannah stood up and paced in front of the neat reception desk.

''It would help if you just told me.'' The gray striped kitten pounced on his thumb, nipping at it and pummeling it with his tiny rear paws.

''It was my agent.''

''Yeah?''

''The local Madison TV station wants me to do one cooking demo each week for the next three months. A local dairy company called and wanted to be my sponsor. It won't be much as far as money, but I'll get free advertising for my cookbooks and my syndicated articles. They said they thought the Madison paper and several more in central Wisconsin would pick it up after my spots start airing.'' She sounded like she didn't believe the words she was saying.

''The station told my agent that they had received more mail, more calls and more e-mail over my cooking spot than anything in the last two years.'' Hannah faced him.

''Wow. That's good, isn't it?''

She nodded, then she giggled and giggled some

more. She plumped down into her mother's office chair and roared.

"What?" Guthrie felt his spirits lighten a tiny bit in the face of her laughter. Hannah laughing struck him as irresistible. He felt himself grinning. "What?"

"It's your aunts!" She shook with mirth.

"My aunts?"

Hannah nodded, trying to muffle her laughter. "Everyone loves your aunts!"

Guthrie had a hard time matching up the woman who'd just finished shingling a church roof with the successful cook and writer. Before Hannah had come to Petite, one of the church ladies had mentioned the fact that the pastor's daughter probably wouldn't stay long in their little town, implying that she'd be too good for Petite. The woman had been wrong. Hannah Kirkland could have been stuck on herself, but she wasn't. She was easy to know, good-hearted. He eyed her. And she was pretty—even after a day spent shingling on a roof. Why wasn't she married by now? Were the men in Milwaukee blind, deaf and dumb?

Chapter Nine

Sitting at the small desk in her harvest-gold room at the Cozy Motel, Hannah shut down her laptop computer and rubbed her tired eyes. Late afternoon sunshine glowed through the window curtains. The phone rang. She picked it up.

"Hannah?" Spring asked.

"Yes, I'm here. I got your e-mail and I've been waiting for your call."

"Okay. I've got Doree on the other line already. Let me access her for you, too."

A click. "Hi, the best Midwest cook." Doree's voice sparkled over the phone line.

"Hi." Hannah's fatigue didn't match her younger sister's high spirits.

"Good." Spring took charge. "Tell us what's going on with our parents."

"Well, the house is still at a stand—"

"No! No!" Doree interrupted.

"But," Hannah talked over Doree's words, "I think that may change in the near future. Guthrie's suggested that they agree to a factory-made shell."

"Wonderful," Spring said.

"What's a shell?" Doree asked.

Hannah ignored Doree. It would be good for Doree, teach her not to be such a pest. "Yes, it could be up in twelve hours, then Guthrie and I will finish the inside."

"You and Guthrie? What does that mean?" Doree squealed.

"Hannah," Spring spoke tentatively, "have you decided yet?"

"Will you look into the family records?" Doree urged.

"Hush, Doree. This is Hannah's decision."

Hannah pondered the question one more time. If her mother had a relapse, but still persisted in refusing to pursue her natural relatives, at least, Hannah's conscience would be clear. The fact of Mom's illness settled like a rock over Hannah's lungs. It made her voice come out rough. "We shouldn't leave anything to chance. I'll look for the adoption papers."

"I'm glad that's finally decided," Spring said quietly.

"Great!" Doree exclaimed.

"Thank you, Hannah," Spring said. "How are Mother and Father?"

"They went to Portage for Mom's routine blood check."

"You'll call us if there is any change?"

"You know I would."

"I'm sorry, Hannah. It's just so hard to be far away."

When the three said their good-byes, Hannah sat with the receiver in her hand till the beeping startled her back to reality. The decision had been made. She'd take the first step in finding her mother's natural parents. *Lord, bless this search or end it. I can't see all the way to the end. You must choose.*

After a long afternoon at the computer making some progress on her writing commitments, Hannah faced the fact that she needed to discuss the cooking show with Ida and Edith Thomas. Her agent had the deal signed, sealed and delivered.

She stood and slipped on her sandals. Each day brought the first taping session nearer. Hannah had specified no more live demos to the TV station and had asked Guthrie not to mention the demos to his aunts. She wanted to tell them in her own way, and she couldn't put it off any longer. She'd waited long enough for inspiration on how to approach the eccentric duo. Time to act.

The ladies' humor lay in their spontaneous helpfulness. If Hannah said the wrong thing, she could spoil their natural charm. In effect, she could knock Humpty-Dumpty off the wall and never be able to put the pieces back together again for another amusing cooking demo.

Sighing, she walked into the warm Saturday afternoon and across Front Street to Church. Though the calendar read September, she wore a peach-colored tank top and shorts and enjoyed the heat of the sun on her bare arms and legs. Two little boys pedaled by on bikes. She waved, and they giggled in return. She knocked at the door of the twin sisters' modest white bungalow, but no one was at home.

After only a month in Petite, Hannah didn't need anyone to tell her where they probably had gone. She walked down the quiet block to the little yellow house, which always vibrated with children's voices.

Maybe she'd fare better asking the two ladies in the midst of their family. It would put less pressure on them if it came up in conversation. Following the well-worn path through the overgrown green grass, she heard the sound of children squealing and shouting in the backyard.

She went around the corner of the house and found Lynda, Martha and the aunts sitting on old metal lawn chairs painted a glossy white in the shade of the tall green maples. They were watching the children splash in a blue plastic wading pool.

"Hannah!" Martha waved to her.

"I was in the neighborhood—"

"Hello, dear," Ida greeted her.

"Yes, hello," Edith echoed. "You're always welcome here."

Hannah chuckled as she sat down in the lawn chair where Martha had motioned her. Ida and Edith definitely must have been their mother and father's pets. Wherever the two went, they always felt they were in control.

"Boy, that looks like fun!" Hannah pointed to the

children in colorful swimsuits chasing each other, sliding their feet on the bottom and making the water slosh over the side. Over a week had passed since the day Amber and Hannah had visited the vet and Hannah had received the call from the TV station in Madison. Though her father didn't break the confidentiality of his recent sessions with Billy and Lynda, he let Hannah know that both parties were working toward Billy meeting his children again after his three-year absence.

Martha sighed. "The days of summer will soon be over. Amber's in kindergarten already, and Jenna just began Head Start in Portage three mornings a week."

Ida clucked her tongue. "They grow up so fast."

Edith added, "It was the same with Guthrie's father, then your children, Martha. These precious years go so fast."

Hannah's heart warmed at the love and affection in the faces of the two great-aunts. *So how do I ask them to appear with me in the cooking show? Would they comprehend what I'm telling them? Would they try to take center stage as the "cooks" when their strength lay in the humor they brought to the cooking demo?* Hannah tried to think of a way to bring up the TV station's proposal. "Ida, Edith, there's a question I need to ask you—"

"Hey!" Amber stepped out of the pool and waved to a woman standing hesitantly at the corner of the house. "Hey! You've got my daddy's dog!"

Hannah swiveled and glimpsed a woman dressed like a country and western singer in spangled denim and with a great deal of large blonde hair. The blonde held the Chihuahua Hannah had seen at the vet's office.

Martha stood. "Terri Sue, oh, Terri Sue!" She hurried over to the woman. The little dog yipped.

Hannah recognized the woman's name. This must be Billy's mother. But she seemed too young to be a grandmother. Hannah studied the woman who had been too ashamed to visit her son's wife and children. Hannah's heart rejoiced.

Amber ran after Martha. "Hey! How come you have my daddy's dog?"

Tears in her eyes, Martha turned to Amber. "Dear, this is your daddy's mother."

Wide-eyed and openmouthed, the little girl halted and stared at the woman.

Martha continued, "Amber, this is your grandmother, Terri Sue."

"Hello, Amber." Terri Sue's voice, low and melodic, sounded fearful, yet awed.

Amber leaped into the air. "A new grandma!" The little girl raced to the pool, shouting at the top of her lungs, "We got a new grandma! We got a daddy! Now we got a new grandma! Come on! Come on!"

Hannah felt like clapping.

Jenna and Hunter tumbled out of the pool and nearly collided with Terri Sue as Martha led her toward the lawn chairs. Rising, Lynda hurried to Terri Sue and hugged her.

"Oh, it's so good to see you again!" Ida and Edith chorused. "We've missed you!" They both slipped dainty hankies from skirt pockets and dabbed at brimming eyes.

"I didn't know if it was too soon...." Terri Sue looked at Lynda's face, her eyes lowered apologetically.

"You've always been welcome," Lynda murmured. "I told you that."

Terri Sue gave a little self-conscious shrug and sat down. "I just couldn't stay away any longer." Her words trembled with three years of longing.

Hannah blinked back tears. Her parents would be thrilled with news of this reunion.

Amber stared at Terri Sue. "Do we got a new grandpa, too?"

"No, dear, no grandpa."

"Did he die like our other grandpa?"

Terri Sue took a deep breath. "No, dear, Billy's daddy left a long time ago."

"You mean like our daddy?" Amber asked.

With a broken expression, Terri nodded.

Hannah ached for the woman.

Hunter leaned against Terri Sue's blue-jeaned leg, soaking it, and asked, "What's your dog's name? We got a cat. Her name is Misty."

Terri Sue touched his soft blond curls. "His name is Taco."

"My name's Hunter!" The little boy bounced with each word. "Can I pet him?"

"Yes, Hunter, just be gentle." Her forehead creased as Terri Sue gazed at the children as if they might be snatched from her at any moment.

Hannah yearned to say some reassuring word to Terri Sue. *But I'm just a bystander.*

Hunter reached toward the dog. Taco yipped once. Hunter pulled his hand back.

Terri Sue stroked the little dog's sleek, but roly-poly tan body. "Taco, this is Hunter. Hunter won't hurt you." She took the boy's small hand and stroked Taco's back with it.

"Oooo," Hunter breathed. "He's soft, nice. Hi, Taco."

Terri Sue smiled.

"Are you really our grandma?" Jenna asked, skepticism in her voice.

"Yes," Martha answered, "she's your father's mother."

"Amber got to see our daddy, but I didn't." Jenna pouted. "When do I get to see him?"

Hannah closed her eyes and said a quick prayer for Billy and Lynda's reconciliation. *I hope for the best, Lord, and trust in your love.*

"Can my daddy come to my school?" Amber asked. "We're drawing special pictures for Open House. Can he come, Mommy? Can he?"

Looking a bit shaky, Lynda inhaled deeply. "Why don't you invite Grandma Terri Sue? Daddy might not be able to come."

"Can you come, Grandma Terri Sue? Please!" Amber begged.

"I'll try," Terri Sue replied in her soft, sultry voice.

"You got a bag on your arm," Jenna told her.

Immediately all three children focused with rapt interest on the colorful paper shopping bag.

Terri Sue put Taco on the grass, then reached into the bag. She paused and looked at Lynda. "I took the liberty of…"

Lynda nodded.

With the bag open at her feet, Terri Sue smiled and drew out three boxed toys—a fashion doll, a creative dough set with bright yellow, green and hot pink dough along with an intriguing collection of shaping forms and a blue toy pickup truck.

Amber shrieked, "It's a Country Western Tammy doll!"

With wide eyes, Jenna asked, "Is the Play-Clay set for me?"

"A truck! Like Uncle Guthrie's!" Hunter danced up and down with excitement.

The children fell onto the toys and ripped open the packages. Then they each took turns hugging Terri Sue and displaying the toys to Martha, the two great-aunts, Lynda and Hannah.

Hannah wished she had a camera to record all the joy in the faces around her.

Then Hunter took his truck into the pool where it plowed through water to the tune of the little boy's expert engine noises. Amber and Jenna retired to the small shaded picnic table to play with the doll and play-clay.

"That was so sweet of you," Ida and Edith crooned.

Terri Sue blinked her richly mascaraed eyes, then dug into her purse for a lavender tissue to blot tears.

"I'm glad you came, Terri Sue. Really." Lynda offered Terri Sue her hand. "I've missed you."

Terri Sue reached out and clung to Lynda's hand. "Oh, honey, I've missed you, too."

"You didn't have to stay away," Martha murmured, sounding close to tears.

Again, Hannah's mind drifted to Lila's monologue. She had mentioned a funeral and Guthrie's father. Billy had done something terrible that had yet to be revealed to Hannah. Had Garner been told everything?

"Billy says you two are going to counseling with the new pastor," Terri Sue said softly and sat back, releasing Lynda.

"Yes. Terri Sue, this is the pastor's daughter, Hannah." Martha made the introduction, apologizing for its tardiness, then stared into the distance as though peering deep into the past.

Terri Sue looked surprised. "Oh, you're the one who did that cooking show."

"Yes." Hannah spoke, glad of the opening this comment gave her. She could say what she'd come for and also lighten everyone's mood. "And I'll be doing it again. The TV station called and wants me to do one a week for the next three months."

"That's so exciting!" Ida and Edith exclaimed. "And to think that we were there to help you the first time!"

"It is exciting!" Hannah agreed. "And I hope you

ladies will come for the show just like you did the last time. You added so much...liveliness to my demo.''

The twin octogenarian sisters looked like they would explode with joy. "Well, if you really want us," Ida said with a coy expression.

"I do. Mark your calendar for this coming Wednesday. A crew is going to come to tape a month's worth of spots at the church starting about nine.''

"We'll look forward to it!"

Lord, I don't know if this is going to work out. Please be there on Wednesday, too!

Déjà vu described the situation on Wednesday. The same director-producer and cameraman had arrived and set up in the institutional-looking kitchen in the church basement. Almost the same group of retired farmers and wives filled the short rows of folding chairs. Ida and Edith sat in the front row on the aisle. Hannah waved to them. They waved back.

"All right, Ms. Kirkland. Let's get started." The producer motioned to her.

Hannah smiled into the camera. "Good day. I'm Hannah Kirkland. I write the 'Real Food, Healthy Food,' column and cookbooks. I like to take America's favorite foods and give them a healthy new twist—without losing a bit of their wonderful taste! Today, I'm going to give you a new quick bread recipe, a variation on an all-time American favorite, banana bread. Mine is Apple-Banana-Oatmeal Bread. A yummy quick bread to go with Johnson's Dairy cream cheese or butter!''

Hannah held up a bunch of bananas. ''Now the best bananas for bread are, of course, the riper ones with brown spots like these. Also fall apples are just coming into the farmers' markets and orchard stores.'' She gestured toward a peck of red apples on the counter to her far right. ''McIntosh or Jonathans are the best for cooking in my opinion. We don't grow bananas here, but no one can beat our apples!''

The church audience applauded.

Hannah set the bananas down and lifted a round blue box of oatmeal. ''And we know that oatmeal along with a healthy diet can lower cholesterol. Besides I love oatmeal! It makes a yummy addition to any quick bread.''

She looked expectantly at the audience. Now to get her comic relief on camera. ''Ida and Hannah, you were so helpful last time. Would you come up and give me a hand today?''

Ida and Edith both smiled sweetly as they apologetically shook their heads.

What! Shock froze Hannah's vocal cords. She struggled to keep a calm mask on her face. ''Okay…then,'' she stammered. Maybe if she continued with the recipe, they'd come up without an invitation. ''This recipe, which makes two standard-sized loaves, begins with two cups of mashed ripe bananas—''

''Cut!'' The producer approached her. In a low voice, he said, ''The two old ladies have *got* to be in this or the dairy company is going to be disappointed. We don't want to disappoint the sponsor, do we?''

"I'm with you all the way," Hannah whispered back passionately. "My dilemma is how to get them up here without spoiling their spontaneity. They've got to come up on their own!"

"I get it. But do they get it? Maybe they don't like to make banana bread."

"Maybe. Maybe not. Just follow me on this, all right? I'll get them up here if I have to pull them bodily into camera range."

The producer gave her a searching look, then nodded and walked out of camera range.

Okay, Lord, I know you're here watching over me. How can I get them up here? I need some inspiration—quick!

In her place behind the kitchen counter, she plastered a broad smile on her miserable face.

"Take it from the top," the producer barked.

Hannah went through the introduction to the recipe again. When she came to the part where she said, "This recipe begins with two cups of mashed ripe bananas," the clear glass bowl that contained the premeasured mashed bananas slipped from her hands and clattered to the counter. The gooey brown bananas shot up and splattered onto Hannah's apron. She zipped off the skins of three more ripe bananas from the bunch she'd displayed and dropped them into another clear glass bowl. When she started to mash the bananas with a potato masher, sharp pain arced through her wrist. "Oh! Ouch!" Dropping the potato masher, she clutched her wrist. Days of pounding nails must have strained it.

"Oh, dear!" Ida exclaimed.

"Oh, dear!" Edith repeated.

The two ladies hurried forward.

Ida took Hannah's hand and examined her wrist. "Edith, I'll take care of her wrist while you mash those bananas! I don't care what Martha says. It's obvious this girl needs us!"

Edith nodded. While she attacked the bananas, mashing them into pulp, Ida reached into the freezer and brought out a blue cloth freezer pack, which she wrapped around Hannah's wrist. "Edith and I bought these for the church to keep on hand. A person never knows when some mishap will come and a ready ice pack can be a godsend."

"You're right," Hannah said, her heart doing handstands. "I feel better already." She did feel better, now that the aunts were on camera with her. What was a strained wrist, after all?

"The bananas are mashed," Edith announced.

"Excellent." Hannah grinned. *Wonderful! Thank you, Lord! I would never have appealed to their sympathy.* "Well, since I'm incapacitated, I'll have to depend on you two to do the mixing. Now to the bananas, add two apples, chopped." Hannah pointed to the prepared and measured ingredients in glass custard cups and bowls. "In a separate small bowl, add four tablespoons water to the fruit and put it aside."

Ida hovered over Hannah like a doting mother hen while Edith followed Hannah's directions.

Hannah finished, "Finally stir in one-half cup golden raisins."

"Do they have to be golden, Hannah?" Ida asked.

Hannah nearly chuckled. *Yes, Ida, that's what the dairy wants to hear!* "No, I suppose you could use the regular dark raisins. I just think the golden raisins look prettier in slices of the bread."

"Oh, yes," Edith agreed. "Our dear mother always said food should be as appetizing to the eye as to the tongue."

Hannah grinned as wide as her mouth permitted.

"Hannah, I don't want to put myself forward, but could we substitute nuts?" Edith asked. "I do love nutmeats in my fruit breads."

Fantastic comment, Edith. Hannah beamed at her. *You, go, girl!* "Oh, yes, walnuts would be an excellent addition. Well, ladies, shall we take the finished loaf out of the oven?"

"Yes!" Ida cooed.

"If you please, Edith?" Hannah motioned toward the country-blue quilted pot holders, which Edith used to open the oven and lift out the warm loaf.

"Oh, the fragrance of the apples!" Ida exclaimed.

"It's like being in an apple orchard!" Edith agreed.

"Cut! That's a wrap," the producer called with obvious relief.

Thank you, Lord! We made it!

"Hello, Hannah."

Her pulse gave a little skip as Hannah recognized Guthrie's voice and his evident unhappiness over the phone. They hadn't spoken for many days. He'd been busy haying, and her parents were still deciding whether to go with the factory shell or not. "What is it, Guthrie?"

"How's your arm?"

"Fine. The pain went away right after the tapings."

"Good. Are you free tonight?"

Why would Guthrie Thomas call and ask her that? The man acted like he was inviting her to a dentist appointment. "I'm just reading a new novel."

"Oh, good." He sounded relieved. "I need you to come to Amber's Open House with me."

"What?"

He sucked in a lot of air before answering. "Lynda says I can't come unless you come with me."

"Why?"

"She says if you aren't there, I might do or say something about…Billy that could embarrass her and the kids."

Hannah pondered this. Evidently, Lynda was open to giving her husband a second chance, but Guthrie still hadn't budged. For this reason and many others, she didn't want to be dragged in as Guthrie's chaperone. "Why don't you just ask my parents to go with you?"

"Lynda says our family is already gossip for miles around. If we have to take a pastor with us to the school to keep peace, she'll die of embarrassment."

"But I'm the pastor's daughter." *And I don't want to be a buffer between you and your ex-brother-in-law.*

"She says that's okay. Everybody knows you helped me with the church roof and had the great-aunts on your cooking show."

Hannah tried to follow this convoluted reasoning, but couldn't. She wasn't surprised. In cases like these, reason rarely controlled action. She let out a deeply sincere sigh. "All right. If Lynda wants me there, come and get me."

"I'll leave now." Click.

Trying to remember what her parents had worn to school functions, Hannah shrugged out of her jeans and red-and-white Badgers T-shirt and slipped into one of her new suits—the peach silk with the creamy white silk blouse. She was just slipping on tan dress shoes when Guthrie tapped on her door.

"Guthrie, are you sure you want me—"

"Let's go."

She shook her head. Single-minded. Stubborn.

Within minutes, Guthrie drove into the crowded school parking lot and maneuvered into a spot at the rear. They'd barely exchanged two words. Looking like a man nursing a broken tooth, he came around to help her out of the cab.

Guthrie wore a pair of casual tan twill slacks and a navy knit sport shirt, which stretched over his wide chest and around bulging biceps. An attractive but glum escort for the evening. *Lighten up, Guthrie!*

Twilight glowed around them. Locusts and crickets harmonized in the fall evening. Suddenly she wanted to pull Guthrie away from the school and wander over to the deserted playground. How long had it been since she'd sat in a swing? She imagined sitting on the wooden board while Guthrie pushed her forward. She'd fly skyward, then backward to Guthrie's strong arms. They would leave behind the family tensions and just enjoy being together.

"We really don't have to go if you don't want to," she offered.

"Nothing is going to make me miss this."

Not encouraged, but unwilling to make a fuss, she took his arm. She quickened her pace as he led her through the school door, then to Amber's kindergarten room. The buzz of voices hummed in the hallways, but zoomed in volume when they walked into the classroom.

Admiring the gaily colored room, Hannah glanced around looking for familiar faces. Several people looked more than a little surprised at seeing them. Was it because they'd come together?

Oh, dear, have I caught the interest of the county gossips? I'll have to make sure everyone knows I'm here only as a family friend!

"Hannah! Hannah!" Amber hailed her, the little girl's high-pitched voice cut through all other voices. "Uncle Guthrie, over here! My picture is on this wall!"

Hannah waved, then found it necessary to cling to Guthrie's arm as he nudged his way through the crowded schoolroom.

Evidently, this was a supportive community of extended families. People of all ages, from great-grandmothers leaning on canes to babes in arms had come to admire the kindergarten members of their families.

Amber was surrounded by every one of her relatives, including her new family, Grandma Terri Sue and Billy. Amber ran the last few steps and grabbed Guthrie's hand and tugged them forward—right up to Billy. "Look, Uncle Guthrie! My daddy came to Open House!"

Feeling like the end of a crack-the-whip game, Hannah swung in front of Guthrie, who gripped her hand almost painfully. She stumbled against Guthrie's broad chest, then steadied herself. "Hello, Billy. It's so nice to meet you. I'm Hannah Kirkland."

Sensing Guthrie fuming behind her like a dormant volcano threatening to erupt, Hannah smiled.

"She's the preacher's daughter, and she writes cookbooks!" Amber announced to the universe.

While shaking Billy's hand, Hannah held on to her smile. This was Amber's night, and Hannah didn't want anything to spoil it. A little child's very first school open house should not be marred by family conflict. She gave Guthrie's hand a warning squeeze.

"Is this your picture, Amber?" Hannah indicated a painted length of newsprint hanging in a row with other pictures.

"Yes, we were supposed to draw a picture of our family. See? Here's the two great-aunties and my grandma Martha." Amber pointed out three stick figures, two with gray hair and wearing dresses and one with yellow hair and apparently wearing slacks. "Over here is Jenna and Hunter and me—we're playing on our swing set.'' Three small stick figures, one with braids, swung on adjoining swings.

"Then, see, I added my new grandma, Terri Sue, my daddy and Mommy.'' Amber had drawn Terri Sue holding what must be Taco and her father and mother holding hands in the middle of the rest of the family.

"Oh! I forgot!'' the little girl exclaimed. She pointed at another couple in the corner of the large piece of paper—a man with yellow hair and large bumps on his stick arms and a woman with short brown hair who was wearing overall shorts. This pair of figures floated above a very pointed green church roof. "And here's you and Uncle Guthrie.''

"But, Amber, I'm not a member of your family,'' Hannah objected, feeling a twitch of nervousness.

"But if you marry Uncle Guthrie, then you'll be my aunt Hannah. Jenna and I want you to be our auntie.''

"Yeah!'' Hunter piped up from his perch on his father's arm.

Several nearby parents, still strangers to Hannah, chuckled at this. Since Amber talked loud enough to be heard by any aircraft flying overhead, Hannah couldn't hold them guilty of eavesdropping. She cringed with embarrassment. "But, Amber, your uncle and I are just friends.''

"But we want you to marry Uncle Guthrie.'' Jenna spoke as loudly as her sister. "Now that our daddy's came back, Uncle Guthrie can get married.''

Hannah didn't like the direction this was leading. She shut her mouth tight and began edging away.

Martha tried to hush the children.

But Amber wasn't taking direction. She put her hand on one hip. "Don't you see? Uncle Guthrie couldn't get married when our daddy was gone because he had to take care of us *like* a daddy. But now we don't need him as our daddy."

Chapter Ten

A few days later, out of the passenger window of Guthrie's truck, Hannah gazed at the gray clouds layered over the slate sky. Her parents had finally agreed to go with the factory-made shell, and she and Guthrie were on their way to order it from the company in Prairie du Chein along the Mississippi River. A sideways glance informed her that this morning's dreary weather matched her companion's mood. His healthy Nordic good looks didn't match the gloom that dragged down the lines of his face.

How she longed to lean close to him, cradle his cheek and comfort him.... But he was unapproachable.

Where had the real Guthrie Thomas gone? Billy's return had flipped a switch somewhere deep inside him. Guthrie the lighthearted but stubborn had given way to Guthrie the angry and wounded. Who could have guessed—except Martha—that this side of Guthrie existed?

As it had over the past few days, the night of Open House came up in Hannah's mind. Poor, sweet little Amber had announced to everyone in hearing distance that she and her brother and sister didn't need Guthrie as a daddy anymore.

The poignant scene had etched itself on Hannah's heart. The sensation of the moment still dogged her. Her blood had drained toward her feet, leaving her clammy and light-headed. Lynda's face had turned a bright red. People had shifted away from them. But Billy had calmly squatted in front of his two daughters. "Amber and Jenna, I know you mean well, but it isn't for you to tell people who to marry or not to marry. That's between Hannah and Guthrie."

Between Hannah and Guthrie.

Right now all that lay between Hannah and Guthrie was a thick buffer of thorny silence. Hannah knew that Guthrie's anger wouldn't get better until it was lanced like an infected wound. But how could she get Guthrie to open up? He'd shut down that evening and hadn't taken any of the hints she offered over the intervening days. In the not-too-distant past, she'd let Edward stonewall her, and it hadn't done either of them any good. Guthrie had to comprehend the damage anger and resentment could do to those he loved and to his own stubborn heart. This could not go on. She wouldn't let it!

Whispering a prayer, she faced Guthrie. "Stop the truck."

"What?" He squealed to a halt, quickly pulling off the road onto the shoulder. "Why?"

She folded her arms over her breast.

"Did you forget something?" When she didn't reply, he demanded, "What? What's wrong?"

Guthrie, listen to yourself! Nothing used to upset you like this.

He fumed at the windshield. "Tell me or I'm driving on."

"Guthrie, I don't think we can go on until you are ready to talk about Billy."

"I'm not talking about Billy." With a glance over his left shoulder, he gunned the truck onto the two-lane highway.

A fleeting flashback brought Edward to mind again. Whenever they'd had a disagreement, he'd iced over like a snow sculpture. To restore peace, she'd had to wheedle and cajole. *I'm not doing that again! Never again!*

This was a perfect opportunity, away from Petite, to get things out in the open. But how could she corner Guthrie? He sat quite literally in the driver's seat.

She stared out as the panorama of late summer Wisconsin ribboned by. Even the clouds that hung overhead like dingy sheets hiding the sun couldn't dim the countryside's simple beauty. Already harvested hay in huge rolls dotted the fields. There were clumps of pine trees and maples gathered in clumps along the roadside. In the highest maples, red-tinged leaves, a harbinger of the inevitable fall, highlighted the rich lingering greens of summer. A blue road sign announced, Wayside, 1/2 Mile on Rt.

Aha! Guthrie couldn't refuse her a pit stop, could he? "I have to stop at the Wayside."

"We'll be in a town in just—"

"I have to stop at the Wayside," she repeated. "It's urgent."

Though still silent, his fuming got louder. But he turned into the Wayside, a grassy, shaded place with picnic tables under shelters, brick facilities and an old-fashioned pump for water.

As soon as he shoved the truck into park, she snatched his keys from the ignition and darted from the vehicle. She didn't stop until she reached a dark green picnic table. She plopped down on the attached bench, her back to the table. There was more than one way to skin a cat or a pigheaded carpenter!

Guthrie stared after her, then stormed out of his truck. When he reached her, he planted his hands on his hips. "What's the bee in your bonnet?"

"You are the bee in my bonnet, Guthrie." She casually crossed her tanned legs and smiled into his stormy face. "We need to talk this out."

"Give me back my keys." He towered over her, a gentle giant in blue jeans.

She shook her head and leaned her elbows on the table. Sitting on Guthrie's wad of keys couldn't be termed comfortable, but she resisted the urge to squirm on the hard bench. She waited.

He took a deep breath. "We have an appointment in Prairie du Chein."

"Then why don't you sit down and we'll get this settled and be on our way."

"Where are my keys?" he demanded through gritted teeth.

"In my shorts."

Leaning down, he reached for her pocket.

She didn't try to stop him. Instead, she gave him an amused smile, the clean scent of his shaving lotion and soap filling her head. "I said in my shorts. Not in the pocket of my shorts."

Taking a step back, he glared at her. "Why are you doing this?"

Her sympathy stirred, she folded her arms. Only deep love for his family and deep pain could have caused such a change in this man. She sighed. "Guthrie, I really like you. You are a great guy. You have a warm heart, and it's as big as Wisconsin. But you are as stubborn as an old mule. Now please spend just a few minutes talking out what's in your mind and heart about Billy coming back into your sister's life. Then I'll gladly give you back the keys."

He turned his back to her.

She waited, praying silently for wisdom. She spoke softly, tenderly. "Guthrie, we're friends. Your well-being is my concern."

Sparrows chirped around them. The din of grasshoppers created a constant background noise. Trucks sped past with their distinctive charged whine.

Finally, Guthrie slumped down beside her.

She touched his arm. "Let me help you. You've helped me and my parents."

"How have I helped you?" He sounded defeated.

"You let me work with you—even if it starched your shorts," she teased. "You convinced my parents to go with the factory-built shell so they wouldn't have to stay at Lila's for months and months. You really care about *us*."

He folded his arms and stared away from her. "I just don't want him here."

Guthrie's troubled capitulation saddened Hannah. But if any tender shoot of healing was to sprout, someone had to start the spadework in this sweet man's wounded heart. "I'm afraid you'll destroy your relationship with your sister."

"Why can't Lynda see he hasn't changed?" He wouldn't meet her eyes.

"How do you know that? Can you look into his heart?"

"I don't have to."

"Guthrie, you're not listening."

He turned to look into her eyes, his forlorn gaze wrenching her heart. "Why can't I make her see reality?"

Again the urge to stroke his cheek, to put her concern into a comforting touch, zigzagged through her. "Guthrie, you can't.... No one can make another person think or feel something they don't want to. Lynda seems to be accepting the changes she sees in Billy, and she's helping the children adjust. You're going to have to stop pushing your own feelings onto your sister."

"She's falling for a lie."

"If you don't stop this, you'll lose her." Hannah recalled how Edward's inflexibility had pushed her further and further away. Until they had moved so far apart, at last, nothing good that had connected them remained. "That would kill you."

A pause. Then he nodded, but his neck moved like it hadn't been oiled in a while.

"So talk to me," she pleaded. "You told me some of why you don't like Billy. And you're right—what he did was awful. But you've got to get rid of your anger and start at giving him a second chance. I can tell my dad thinks Billy has experienced a true change of heart, and my dad isn't usually fooled."

"People like him don't change." He spoke as though each word had to be dragged up from deep in his soul. "He'll just end up hurting them again."

"Guthrie, with God's help people do change." She pursed her lips, then continued, "I know you want to protect your sister and her children, but you're not God."

"I don't think I'm God."

"You do if you think it's in your power to prevent your sister from being hurt. You can't. If Lynda wants to let Billy begin to act like a father to his children, that's good—even if it poses emotional danger to her and the kids."

"I thought Billy was in the past. I didn't expect to see him again."

Again the memory of Lila's mention of a funeral, of Guthrie's dad nagged her. Did she dare bring this question up now? A glance at Guthrie's bleak expression told her no. "Give him a chance."

"I'll try." Abruptly, Guthrie stood up.

His sudden agreement didn't sound genuine. Was he agreeing just so they could get on to their destination? Or had some little part of him decided to give Billy another chance? She looked up, studying his honest blue eyes, which plainly warred with his clenched jaw. But she could only take Guthrie's word. She wasn't God, either.

"Keys?" He held out his hand.

She rose, and the bunch of keys fell out of the right leg of her pale pink shorts and made a tinny chink on the concrete. Bending, Guthrie snatched them and started across the green grass.

She trotted at his side, or tried to. "I'm glad you're going to give Billy a second chance."

Guthrie jogged toward the truck. "Come on. We're going to be late for our appointment."

"I'm glad you are giving him a second chance because we're double-dating Saturday night."

"What!" he bellowed, swinging back to her.

"Gotcha!" she teased, then went on more seriously, "now remember how we told my mom and dad we'd help with the singles' party at the church this weekend? Well, both your sister and Billy said they'd come, so you need to figure out how you're going to deal with that."

Looking grim, Guthrie stared at her.

"Don't worry." She patted his cheek daringly. "I

have faith in you. Besides, we'll all be well chaperoned.''

The Twenty-One Plus Night in the neat but beige church basement witnessed the first public reunion between Lynda and Billy. Hannah had agreed to drag Guthrie along to take some of the heat off Lynda and Billy—that is, give Petite something else to talk about.

Hannah hoped this evening would be the first step in reconciling Guthrie to Billy's return. She had done her part to make the evening a success by fixing the refreshments—a new cheese dip with a hint of jalapeños, double fudge brownies and ripe red watermelon chunks.

Her parents had deputized Lynda and Billy to be in charge of entertainment, and they had brought Lynda's portable CD player and a selection of CDs with songs from the fifties and sixties. Good food, classic rock, but bad vibes.

About a dozen young men and women who were casually dressed in shorts and cutoffs and T-shirts and had known each other or known of each other for most of their lives stood around as though they'd never seen each other or the church basement before in their lives. Hannah tried to think of an icebreaker as Lynda whispered to her, ''This is awful. What can we do to get everyone to relax?''

''Good evening, everyone!''

All faces turned to the doorway to witness Ida and

Edith, wearing pink-flowered dresses, make their entrance.

Hannah's mouth dropped open. Lynda murmured, "Oh, my." Glancing at Lynda's face, Hannah saw her own shock reflected there.

Billy hurried forward. "Aunt Ida, Aunt Edith, what brings you here tonight?"

"Well, we're over twenty-one and single!" Ida, with a gleam in her eye, announced. "We came to have fun."

"We've looked forward all week to the party!" Edith agreed.

Ida gazed around at the ill-at-ease group of singles. "And look at all of you, just standing around! We didn't think you youngsters would know anything about party games! Young people today just don't know how to have fun."

"No, indeed. And see—we were right!" Edith added. "Now, Billy, you line up all these handsome young men on one side of the room while Ida and I get all the young ladies lined up opposite them."

For a moment, everyone merely stared at the two elderly ladies. Hannah felt their hesitance. Not party games! The twin octogenarian ladies were clearly out of place, but who could hurt their feelings by saying so?

Evidently no one.

Billy started calling each guy's name, and though somewhat reluctant, all the males lined up alongside Guthrie. The females lined up facing the gentlemen.

Having learned more about the eccentric ladies,

Hannah surmised that no one present could think of a way to refuse the two dear old souls. Everyone present remembered Ida and Edith had first diapered them in the church nursery, then given them Sunday school lessons. And who among them could ever forget the ladies who gave out king-size chocolate bars and cheerful greetings at Halloween?

When the two lines had formed, Ida rearranged the males. Hannah tried to figure out why Ida was doing this. When Ida moved Billy to face Lynda, then Guthrie opposite herself, Hannah got it. The two were shamelessly matchmaking!

Edith came behind her sister, dispensing from a brown shopping bag red-and-white-striped plastic drinking straws and hard candies with holes in the middle like life rings. Each female received a drinking straw, each male a straw and a candy.

When the ladies reached the ends of the lines, they turned and beamed. Ida began, "Now, there will be a prize for the couple who can be the first to transfer the candy from the gentleman's straw to the lady's. The straws must be held in your mouths and hands must remain behind your backs, of course, and no talking allowed!"

"Oh, this is going to be such fun!" Edith tittered. "I remember we did this at our sixteenth birthday party."

"Hush," Ida scolded, then continued, "if you drop a candy, you may have up to two more. If you drop more than three, you will be disqualified. Get ready, get set, go!"

The male and female lines stared at each other.
Then, folding his arms behind him, Billy put the straw
in his mouth, then the candy on his straw, and stepped
toward Lynda. Lynda placed her straw between her
lips and tried to touch the end of her straw to Billy's.

Guthrie gave a disgruntled snort, but followed suit.

Feeling ridiculous, Hannah clasped her hands behind her back and stepped closer to Guthrie. She
thought she recalled doing this at a fourth-grade birthday party. She tried to aim her straw at the end of
Guthrie's. But he was too tall. She made noises and
exaggeratedly nodded down, directing him to bend his
head.

He made negative sounds and flexed his knees a
bit so his straw would be level with hers. She leaned
forward and tried to touch her straw to his. The candy
sailed down his straw. Unaccountably trembling, she
tried to hold the connection. The candy slipped between their straws, shattering on the cement floor.
Hannah couldn't believe it!

Clucking like a mother hen, Ida hurried over with
another candy, which she slipped onto Guthrie's
straw. "Try again!"

Hannah and Guthrie did. All around them was the
hullabaloo of others making noises around straws in
their mouths. Glancing to one side, Hannah glimpsed
Ted, the auto repair shop owner, nearly on his knees
in front of Becky, the youngest hairstylist from Petite's Bizzy Bee Beauty Shop. Their candy dropped.
Ted groaned while Becky burst into giggles.

Guthrie grunted fiercely at Hannah. She gave him

her attention and tried to concentrate on the end of his straw. She wished she could say, "Stop bobbing around, Guthrie, and just kneel down. Then I'll kneel and we won't jiggle so." But of course, she couldn't!

Their second candy took its own sweet time rolling down his straw. Just as Hannah thought she had her straw firmly connected to Guthrie's, the candy slipped between them and hit the floor.

Edith stopped, shaking her forefinger at them. "This is your final candy, Guthrie. Look at each other's faces so you can communicate with your eyes and head. You've got to try harder or you'll never win!"

Hannah took the advice and focused on Guthrie's face. She nodded downward, motioning him to kneel. With his straw pointed toward the ceiling to keep from losing their final candy, he slipped slowly to his knees. She followed suit, then bent her head low. He leaned forward. The straw wavered in front of her eyes, then she glanced to his face. She nearly laughed out loud. His concentration was so intense! She stifled her amusement and held very still.

Their final candy inched its way down Guthrie's straw. Hannah, touching her straw to his, held her breath. The candy slowly, tremulously moved from his straw to hers. It slid down and bumped her lips.

"Guthrie and Hannah win!" Edith and Ida crowed. The sisters presented them each with a super-size candy bar. "Now for the spoon-link race!"

This game involved a race between the two lines. Each line was given a spoon tied to a long string.

"Now," Ida instructed, "each of you must drop the spoon down your neckline and shake it out the bottom of your pant leg. No hands allowed!"

Edith shook her head and frowned. "I must say, if you ladies had worn dresses, you would have found this much easier. And it's good none of you wore those tight blue jeans! But as it is, everyone, please take off any belts, and you may unbutton your waist buttons. Now the team that connects every member in the line with their string first will win!" She handed one spoon to Hannah and one to Guthrie.

Momentarily, they stared at each other, then Hannah dropped the spoon into her kelly-green T-shirt. The cold metal made her shiver and of course the spoon immediately caught in her décolleté. She jumped up and down to dislodge it. The women of her team shouted encouragement. She glanced at Guthrie and saw he was jumping up and down also, trying to get the spoon to slide past his waistband into his cutoffs. She started giggling and couldn't stop. Finally, after she imitated a woman with ants crawling up her leg, the spoon clattered to the floor below her right shorts leg.

Becky snatched it up and dropped it down her neckline. Hannah shouted encouragement and instructions to her. Becky wiggled, jiggled, twisted and shimmied. Finally, it slid to the floor. Lynda grabbed it and shoved it down her neckline. Watching Lynda's gyrations, Hannah screamed with laughter. Everyone in both lines was laughing.

Hannah gasped for breath, then began cheering as her team won. "Yeah! Yeah!"

Looking forlorn, Ted had the spoon dangling from his shirttail. "Not fair! Not fair!" the guys complained.

Ida and Edith shook their heads at the male team but beamed at the ladies. "Well done! Now for our final game—musical chairs!" The twin aunts bullied the guys into setting up a double row of back-to-back chairs with one less chair than was needed. Then they made Lynda show them how to work the CD player.

So to the sound of lively rock and roll, the singles all trooped around the back-to-back line of chairs, anticipating the inevitable stopping of the music. During the fourth round, Hannah landed on Guthrie's lap instead of the chair. For only a second, she processed the shock of feeling Guthrie's hard thighs beneath her. Blushing, she popped up and complained, "He stole my chair!"

Ida and Edith waved her away from the line of chairs. "No sore losers, Hannah!"

After Hannah's elimination, the competition became cutthroat. Several more competitors landed in laps instead of chairs, and teasing accusations of cheating echoed off the church basement walls.

Finally, it was down to Lynda, Billy and Guthrie. To a rocking golden oldie, the trio stalked around in a circle, their fingers never leaving the backs of the two remaining straight chairs, their gazes never leaving the faces of their competitors.

The music stopped.

Guthrie thumped down onto a chair, but Lynda docked on Billy's lap. Guthrie jumped up, fire in his eyes.

"Wonderful!" a voice called.

Hannah turned to see her father and mother enter.

"Wonderful!" her father repeated. "Everyone looks like they're having a great time!"

But what Guthrie whispered in an undertone to Billy caught Hannah's ear and stabbed her heart. "You can make up to my sister all you want, but don't think I'll ever forget what you did to my father."

Chapter Eleven

The last ones left in the church, Hannah and Guthrie were standing side by side in the church kitchen. The lemon scent of dish detergent floated above the sink. Hannah had planned it that way, though she'd practically had to tie him to her leg to keep him from following Billy and Lynda out the door. She couldn't put off talking to Guthrie about the changes she'd seen in him since Billy's return. Hannah handed Guthrie the final dish to dry and stared at him.

The words he'd whispered to Billy still burned in her ears. Whatever Billy had done to Lynda and Guthrie's father in the past was nothing to what it was doing to Guthrie right now. She didn't know if she was the best person to speak, but she couldn't call herself Guthrie's friend and let this go on. She pulled out the drain stopper and watched as the last of the suds was sucked down the drain.

She turned, took the dried dish from Guthrie's hand

and gently pushed him to sit at the small built-in table in the nook of the kitchen. She switched the large overhead light off and sat across from him, only the low light from the nearby stove's range hood illuminating the room. "Guthrie, this has gone on long enough. It's time for you to get rid of the anger and leftover pain that Billy's responsible for. That's the easiest way I can say it. Please tell me everything that happened so you can put it behind you and start being Guthrie again."

He looked stunned, then recovered enough to frown. "I'm still Guthrie," he said in a prickly tone.

"No, you're not. You haven't been the same man since Billy came back to town."

Folding his large hands on the pine table, Guthrie wouldn't meet her eyes.

"Just tell me. I'm your friend. We'll pray about it. Please give it up. Let God start healing your damaged heart." She reached over and slipped her hand between both of his. His rough hands reminded her of what a hardworking, faithful man he was. In the short time she'd known him he had won her respect and liking. "Only God has that healing power. He wants the best for you." *Guthrie, don't fight it anymore.*

He pushed back on his seat and stretched his legs out on each side of hers. He drew in air, then let it out slowly. "You should know the whole story. So you'll understand why he can't be trusted." He made eye contact with her, but only for an instant. "I told you about how Billy stole Lynda's car and the money she'd saved?"

She squeezed his warm hand and nodded.

"My father had cancer…he was dying of it."

Oh, no. What a dreadful combination. "I didn't know that. I just knew that you'd lost him earlier than you had expected." She lay her other hand over his.

Guthrie stared at the wall above her head. "Billy wrecked the car he stole. He was out near our farmhouse. Dad was there with Aunt Ida and Aunt Edith. He'd been too sick to go to the hospital to be with Lynda when she was having Hunter. Billy walked to our farmhouse and hot-wired our old truck."

Hannah closed her eyes and bent her head, the burden of callous sin, not even her own, weighing her down. *How could you, Billy? How could you pile betrayal on top of betrayal?*

"My dad heard the noise and managed to get outside. Aunt Ida said Billy nearly ran my dad down when he tried to stop Billy." Guthrie drew in breath. "I know Dad was already failing, dying, but his last few weeks were made hellish by worry over Lynda…disappointment over how Billy had treated her and the children."

"It multiplied your grief." Hannah tightened her grip on his strong hands.

"It was…awful."

Hannah didn't speak. She waited, giving both of them time to recover from the ordeal of putting Billy's sins into words. She longed to draw Guthrie's hand to her cheek so she could cradle it there, a sign of comfort, sharing.

Finally, she murmured, "But all that is in the past.

Your being angry isn't going to spare your father any pain. He's with God, beyond pain. All the tears have been wiped from his eyes. Don't you think he wants you to be happy? And Lynda and the children?''

"Of course, but I just don't trust Billy.''

"You have to have faith. Faith is things hoped for. Right now, Guthrie, *you've* become the problem.''

"Me?'' He looked aghast, disgruntled.

She nodded. "You're upsetting your whole family. I told you before—you can't control anyone's feelings but your own. You can't stop Lynda from wanting to trust her ex-husband again or Billy from hurting his family again *if* he decides to go back to his old ways.

"All you can do is get out of the way, not *create problems* for Lynda and her family. Don't you think Lynda's children will begin to pick up on your animosity toward their father? How will that affect them? Don't you see that?''

Closing his eyes, he leaned his head back, stretching his neck until the top of his head touched the wall behind him. He finally nodded.

A relieved sigh flowed through Hannah. *Dear God, please let this family, this kind man, have a happy ending.*

Then, when she least expected it, Guthrie increased his pressure on her hands and drew them up to his lips.

Her breath caught in her throat as his lips grazed her knuckles. How could such a powerful man be so tender, so gentle? He stood, pulling her to her feet.

Her gaze never left his face as he drew her closer, closer…and bent his head.

She lifted her face to him.

From outside came the scream of a fire engine. The moment was shattered. She and Guthrie froze in place.

"That sounds awfully close." She thought of her parents, Guthrie's nieces and nephews asleep in this village.

"Let's go!" Guthrie, still holding her hand, hurried through the darkened basement, then outside. In the cooler night air, he didn't break stride. Hannah sprinted to keep up with him. Her concentration was directed to the horizon. It flickered with an unnatural light.

Dear God, it's right on Church or Front Street. Please don't let anyone be injured. Protect the men who are fighting the fire. Her litany of prayers for safety kept pace with her legs. Her heart pounded with fear.

Others from the small town joined the race with them. Ahead, the red lights of one, no, two fire engines turned, splashing their alien glare onto the pavement and the deserted houses. At the corner of Front and Church streets, Guthrie stopped.

Hannah bumped against him. She gasped. "It's the café!"

Hanson's Cozy Café disgorged tongues of flame and billows of coal-black smoke. The mounting smoke obscured the motel. "My parents!" She lurched forward.

Guthrie caught her by both arms. "There! There they are!"

She swung around and followed Guthrie's nod. Her parents stood well away from the fire with Lila by their side. "Mom! Dad! The kittens!" Guthrie released her. She hurried to them and threw her arms around them both.

"Oh, Hannah!" her mother wailed. "We were only able to get the kittens and your laptop out! The smoke, the water will damage everything the fire doesn't destroy! All your beautiful new clothes!"

Not able to speak, Hannah squeezed, her arms stretched around both her parents at once. *Safe! They're all safe, even the kittens! Thank you, God!*

Nearby, her eyes awash with tears, Lila kept moaning, "How could this happen? How?"

Firemen shouted to each other. The engines churned, powering the pumps and lighting the scene. Windows in the motel exploded from the heat. Water hissed as it quenched flame.

Finally, the fire surrendered, drenched into extinction. The café had been demolished by water and flame. The motel stood blackened and empty. The odor of burned wood and melted plastic fouled the air.

Hannah shivered in the dark chill of midnight and folded her arms around herself. Though she'd only brought her writing and clothes with her to Petite, she was experiencing a keen sense of loss, disorientation. *I have no place to go.*

In twos and threes, those who'd come to watch

began drifting to their homes. Everyone stopped to say a word to Lila or to hug her. Ida and Edith insisted that Lila come home with them for the night.

Lila tried to refuse.

But Ida insisted. "No, no, Lila, you shouldn't be alone after something like this. We'll make you a cup of hot chamomile tea, then you can sleep in our guest bedroom upstairs."

"Absolutely. You mustn't be alone," Edith agreed. "We are happy to be able to do something for our neighbor."

Hannah watched the two old ladies lead the disheveled and silent Lila away.

Hannah's father spoke. "Well, it's good we left our car parked at the church. I guess we'd better drive to Portage and see about a hotel room."

"No." Guthrie appeared beside her and her parents. "I've got a whole farmhouse to myself."

Hannah stared at him, his words taking her by surprise.

"Oh, no, we couldn't impose," her mother said.

Guthrie shook his head with no-nonsense determination. "I'm not letting you three go to another motel. Now come on. Hannah's SUV and my truck are still parked at the church." He turned to her. "Are you in shape to drive?"

She nodded, too tired, too shocked at this turn of events to object.

"Then you can drive your parents and follow me out to the farm."

Hannah felt unable to form an opposing opinion.

Too much had transpired in too short a time. Mom had made the right choice in the thing she'd salvaged. The laptop with all her writing on it was the one thing Hannah couldn't do without. But what a feeling! She didn't even have a toothbrush to take to Guthrie's! And did she want to stay in Guthrie's house? At the moment, she didn't have the luxury of choice.

A lowing of cattle woke Hannah. For a few seconds, she couldn't remember where she was. Then scenes from the night before, the Twenty-One Plus Night at church and the fire, cascaded through her mind. She closed her eyes, then with a sigh opened them again.

In the dark early morning hours, Guthrie had led her parents and her up to rooms on the second floor. Her parents had taken the room across the hall from her. After they'd gone into their room, Guthrie had murmured that this room had been his sister's, then left her with a pair of his folded cotton pajamas in her hand. She pictured it like a scene in an old black-and-white movie. The two of them, standing close in the dark hallway, the funny feeling of wanting to move into his arms, but knowing she couldn't.

Hannah got out of bed. Holding up the too-long pajama legs like folds of a long skirt, she walked to the old-fashioned double-hung window. Guthrie's dairy feeder cattle wandered, grazing, spread out over the muted green and golden pastures. The faded pink curtain beside her was soft under her fingertips. She bent her head against the wooden window frame.

How would she and her parents adjust to being, in effect, homeless? It was a peculiar feeling. Lila's Cozy Motel hadn't been a five-star hotel, but it had begun to feel like home. What now? Should she go back to Milwaukee and move in with Spring or to Madison and bunk with Doree? Neither appealed at all. Her parents needed her, and the idea of leaving Guthrie behind left her feeling empty.

Guthrie almost kissed you last night, her conscience whispered. *You shouldn't lead him on when you don't intend to fall in love with him.*

"Too late," she murmured with dawning dismay. *How could I help falling in love with Guthrie?*

You just ended a three-year engagement— Her conscience broke off at a tap on her door.

"Hannah, the coffee's ready down in the kitchen."

Guthrie's voice made her spine tingle.

"All right," she called in a voice that didn't sound quite like her own.

She listened to his footsteps shuffle quickly down the wooden steps. Not having any choice, she shrugged out of the oversize pj's and into her fire-scented shorts outfit from last night and quickly made her bed. She knocked at her parents' door, but found the room empty. Were they downstairs or was she all alone in the farmhouse with Guthrie? Phantom butterflies fluttered their gossamer wings in her stomach.

In the kitchen, Guthrie lounged at the table sipping coffee, alone.

"Where are my mom and dad?" she asked, pausing in the doorway.

He motioned her to help herself to the pot of coffee still warming on the old white porcelain stove. A mug decorated with yellow daisies and a spoon had been set out for her on the nicked Formica counter.

Feeling as self-conscious as a new child in a strange school, she made a wide circuit around him.

"They went to Portage hospital to visit one of the volunteer firemen who was burned last night."

His words startled her. She halted her first sip of the hot coffee. "Was he seriously hurt?"

"No, just some second-degree burns on his face and hands. But he's on oxygen until his lungs clear a bit more. He should be home by tomorrow. Your mom said she'd stop and pick up some clothing and toiletries for you. She said she knew you wanted to write today."

Write today? It was the farthest thing from her mind. Hannah sat across from Guthrie and tried not to stare at him. She'd been alone with this man many times over the past weeks, but had never experienced quite the same sensation. She couldn't take her gaze from him. The gold of his corn silk hair, the way it curled around his ears, the squareness of his determined jaw...

She closed her eyes and took a deep breath. *I've just ended an engagement. I'm vulnerable.* Rebound bait, Doree had called her in a recent phone call. *And I've spent a lot of time with this man. These are just feelings, and they will vanish all by themselves if I ignore them. I'll pack up my stuff from the motel and move into one closer to Portage. That will take care of these... longings.*

She opened her eyes.

Guthrie had leaned forward, his powerful arms resting on the wooden tabletop. "The motel is going to take a lot of cleaning and repairs, and the café will have to be rebuilt. I've invited your mom and dad and now you to stay here while Lila gets everything back in order."

What?

"Your parents said it was fine with them and didn't think you'd have any objection."

Objection? Oh, Guthrie, what am I going to do about you? Or, more importantly, about me? This just isn't a good time for either of us. Why didn't I realize how susceptible I'd be to a warmhearted guy like you?

Over two weeks later, Guthrie watched Hannah drive up and park her SUV on the muddy road near her parents' lot. He stood beyond the construction site and watched the crew from the factory-built-shell company work. A huge crane was poised over the foundation, and the workers were putting up the shell, wall by wall.

"Wow." Hannah walked up beside him. "The windows are in and everything."

He ignored his marked reaction to her. She smelled of vanilla and glowed with energy. If he didn't hold himself in check, he might just pull her into his arms

and kiss her—right here in front of God and everybody. He couldn't keep Hannah out of his thoughts.

Each morning, he found himself lingering in the
kitchen listening for her footsteps on the stairs. Then
she'd sit down with him at the table where he'd eaten
breakfast alone for years. She lit up the room with
her teasing smile and friendly laughter.

That evening after the Twenty-One Plus Night
party, he'd intended to kiss her. That is, he hadn't
intended to, but he almost had. Nothing had gone the
way he'd anticipated since then.

More and more, Lynda had been letting Billy hang
around her and the kids. Everyone seemed to think
that Billy was a new man. They might be right, but
the fear of history repeating itself still had the power
to make Guthrie nervous. Hannah had been right, too.
He could do nothing to prevent his sister from letting
Billy into her life and in the process make what might
prove the second biggest mistake of her life.

All Hannah had said that night in the church
kitchen made sense, but he still couldn't quite shake
the feeling that Billy couldn't be trusted with the
heavy responsibility of fatherhood. Billy might think
he could, but he might bite off more than he could
chew. Yet hard as it was, Guthrie had held his tongue.

And Hannah… He'd let himself get too close to
her. Hannah Kirkland had irritated him more than
once, but he'd liked her right away. Everyone did.
But she had this way of sticking her nose into his
business. She'd insisted on helping him with the
church roof out of concern for her parents. She'd spo-

ken to him about Billy fearlessly and honestly. Who could stay mad at a kind-hearted, dark-haired, lovely...

"Oh, this is so exciting! I wouldn't have believed it if I hadn't seen it with my own eyes." Hannah's voice sounded her wonder. "The shell really will be up in twelve hours."

"Maybe less." He kept his tone noncommittal. The crane creaked as it swung another wall into place. How could he help noticing that the woman beside him bubbled over with vitality and charm? "You're looking good today." He couldn't have stopped the words if he'd been struck dumb.

"Oh?" She blushed.

Why had he said that to her? Hannah Kirkland was a writer. She was on TV. She wouldn't be interested in him, a small-town carpenter, a farmer in deep debt. Besides, he'd given up on love long ago when...*she'd* left. Then his father had gotten sick. Billy had... He pushed away the unhappy memories. Today was a happy day. Finally, this summer, something good was happening.

"After you left this morning, I got two calls." She spoke to him, but her eyes never strayed from the activity yards in front of them.

"Oh?"

"First my sister Spring called to say she would be coming to visit. Would you mind if she bunked in with me a couple of nights?"

"That'll be fine."

"And the county fair chairwoman called to ask me

to judge the pie competition at the county fair along with your great-aunts.''

''Oh?''

''That's the news.'' She turned to him with a smile bright enough to light up Milwaukee.

He grabbed at the safe topic she'd offered him. ''It's hard to believe it's time for the county fair. It always means the real end of summer.''

''Yes, and fall always flies by. You've got all your hay in?''

He nodded. ''Yeah, and that's a real blessing. I won't have to pay for feed for my cattle this winter. They'll be fat and ready to sell to dairies come spring without huge feed bills.''

And though he hadn't believed it would happen, Billy had started giving Lynda money each week. It wasn't enough so she could quit work and stay home with the kids, but it was enough to pay the groceries and a few bills. Not having to help Lynda as much allowed Guthrie to start paying off his debts faster than he'd anticipated. Even though he'd argued against it, the Kirklands were pitching in for groceries and bills at the farm.

Then Billy had tried to give him a check to help pay off the debt for Hunter's birth. Though Guthrie had refused Billy's check, telling him to give it to Lynda, it had felt good this month when Guthrie had been able to write a healthy figure on the principal line of the bank mortgage form.

Hannah turned halfway from him. ''I hope we're

not crowding you at the farm. We can always move out.''

"No, not at all.''

"But you might need our rooms. Your mom says your brother called today.''

"Brandon?'' Guthrie couldn't remember the last time his brother had communicated with them.

"Yes, he's coming for a visit.''

Guthrie snorted. "She must have heard him wrong. He never leaves San Francisco.''

"No, I'm sure she said Brandon's trying to come in time for the county fair. And he wants to stay at the farm. I'll be happy to move out.''

A spark ignited Guthrie's temper. "No. You're staying. He can get a room at a motel in Portage or bunk with Aunt Edith and Aunt Ida. They'll enjoy having him.''

"But your mom said—''

"He'll stay in town. Brandon never had any use for the farm.'' *Is Deirdre coming with him?* Guthrie felt a little sick at the possibility.

Under cover of the worn county fair marquee, open on all four sides, Hannah stood between Ida and Edith. The sweet scent of fruit pies wafted all around them and blended with the smell of warm canvas in the late September afternoon breeze. "Ladies, it looks like we have our work cut out for us.''

They were surrounded by long tables covered with row after row of golden pies—cherry, apple, blueberry, peach, blackberry, strawberry, rhubarb and more, many more. Outside, gray clouds layered the sky, promising rain.

"I hadn't thought there would be so many entries," Hannah murmured, feeling like a piece of pastry dough that had just been flattened by a heavy rolling pin.

"It will be quite a challenge," Ida agreed, sporting an old-fashioned full apron in pink-and-white gingham.

"But we know how to do it." Edith, wearing a matching apron, nodded.

"What do you suggest?" Hannah bent over and propped one elbow on the front table. Right now, tasting pies ranked dead last in what she wanted to do.

"We start by looking at each pie."

"Judging for appearance?" Hannah guessed.

"Of course, dear." Ida smiled primly. "A good-tasting pie rarely looks bad, at least in a contest, you know. The cook wouldn't bring anything less than the very best."

"After we look, then we taste." Edith finished with a knowing grin.

So Hannah began, but as she judged she watched the ebb and flow of familiar faces around the centrally located pie-judging area. Part of her mind watched for Spring to arrive. Her parents had promised to bring her directly to the fair when she arrived. The other part of her concentrated on pie appearance, pastry texture, filling flavor. She marked these on her scorecard, as did the aunts.

But Hannah had to admit there was one face she

was watching for even more than Spring's—Guthrie's. She had to turn this Guthrie trend around. Between Billy's return, Mom's health and the wait to look for the adoption papers, there was a great deal at stake in their families. She had to get over Guthrie and fast.

After the pies had been judged by the visual criterion, Hannah's vigil for her sister ended. Flanked by their parents, Spring, wearing an ivory linen shift, stopped and goggled at all the pies. "You're not really going to taste all these pies, are you?"

"I'm so happy to see you, too." Hannah's mouth twisted into a wry grin. She stepped outside the judging area.

"Oh, I'm sorry, Hannah." Spring hugged her sister and whispered, "I saw the house. It won't be long and you'll be in."

"No problem." Hannah gave her sister a special smile of understanding.

After meeting the aunts, Spring and their parents wandered away with Martha, who had Amber and Jenna in hand, and Hannah returned to the rows of pies.

At long last, Hannah, Ida and Edith finished the tasting and bestowed the ribbons on the top three pies. Hannah collapsed onto a lawn chair beside the pie tent. Carnival music accompanied the sound of shots from the target game and the ping of quarters tossed at jars. The buttery smell of popcorn and the sweet smell of cotton candy wafted on the increasing breeze. Crowds soon clogged the fairground walkways. Lynda and Billy with Hunter stopped to chat. Hannah smiled at seeing the three of them enjoying the fair together.

"Daddy," Hunter insisted, "I want a corn dog!"

"Okay, okay." Billy ruffled Hunter's mop of blond hair. "We'll be right back, Mom."

"Just one," Lynda called after them. "He's already had cotton candy and a funnel cake!"

Hannah, certain she'd eaten the equivalent of two whole pies, felt a little queasy. "Please don't talk about food."

Lynda laughed. "Pie contest get to you?"

Hannah noticed that Guthrie's sister looked even prettier than she had when they'd met. An inner glow had begun to glimmer in her eyes and expression.

Spring, clutching a white bear almost half her size, returned with Garner and Ethel. "Look, Father pitched quarters and won me a bear!"

Hannah made herself pout. "I want a bear, too."

Dad laughed.

Guthrie made his way through the crowd. Stopping near them, he smiled at her.

Her heart did a flip-flop, but Hannah covered it with a friendly wave to him. "Why weren't you here earlier? We needed help judging those pies."

"I was judging rabbits for the 4-H kids."

Hannah introduced him to her sister.

"Nice to meet you, Spring." He nodded.

"Rabbits!" Spring exclaimed. "They're my favorite!"

"Me, too. I love the ones with the lop ears, so

unusual.'' Behind them, Ida cut a generous piece of blueberry pie, put it on a paper plate and handed it to Guthrie.

''Yes, dear, eat,'' Edith encouraged. ''You look tired.''

Guthrie chuckled, then bit into the blueberry pie.

''Let me guess.'' Hannah rested her index finger on the side of her chin. ''Blueberry is your favorite.''

A drop of the purple juice and a berry slid down his chin. Hannah nearly reached out to catch them with her fingertip. She gave herself a little shake.

''Lynda! Lynda!'' Billy shoved his way to his wife, who had reached up to wipe her brother's chin. ''Is Hunter with you?''

''No.'' Concern leaped onto Lynda's face.

''He was right with me. I reached up for our corn dogs. I turned around and he was gone.''

Chapter Twelve

"**D**on't panic. We'll find your boy," Hannah's father said, his face stern. "Hannah, do you have your new cell phone?"

Still stunned, Hannah slid it out of her pocket.

"Call nine-one-one. I'm sure I saw a deputy around here. I want the county sheriff right now. I think the little guy has just got himself lost, but these days we can't take any chances."

As her father talked, Hannah punched the numbers in. Her hands trembled. Had Hunter become lost in the crowd or had he been snatched by a stranger? When a voice answered, she handed the phone to her father.

With few words, he told the dispatcher the problem and hung up. "Now, Guthrie and Bill, there are only two parking lots. Bill, you take the north lot. Guthrie, you take the west. Gather a few friends as you go. The sheriff said to refuse to let anyone leave. His orders.'' Guthrie and Bill raced off in different directions.

Dad turned to his wife, Hannah, Spring and Lynda. "I'm going to go to the man in charge of the public address system, so he can broadcast an alert for Hunter. The four of you take different areas, search for Hunter and spread the word.'' He gave Lynda a quick hug. "Don't worry. God is with him and with us. We'll find him. Now go.''

Grateful to be able to help, Hannah hurried away, her heart racing. Visions of forlorn faces of lost children on posters and milk cartons filled her with icy terror. She tried to reason with her fear. Children got confused in crowds and wandered away all the time, but her urgency to search for Hunter didn't wane. As she hurried along examining every nook, she watched for familiar faces. She saw Lila coming toward her. "Lila, Hunter's lost! Have you seen him?''

"No—''

The public address system crackled to life. "Attention. Hunter Garrett, a four-year-old boy with blond hair, has come up missing. He is wearing blue jeans and a Packer T-shirt. If you see him, please bring him to the central judge's station. Thank you.''

Lila rushed to catch up with Hannah. "I'll help you. Lynda must be frantic.''

Hannah nodded, but concentrated on searching for a little towheaded boy in a Packer T-shirt. Each minute, each step made her heart thump harder. *Dear Lord, please help us find him. Comfort Lynda and Billy. Don't let anyone hurt Hunter.*

The minutes roared passed. Everywhere people, strangers and friends, were calling, "Hunter! Hunter!" Two sheriff's cars drove into the fairground and blocked the exits. Hannah welcomed the blare of their sirens and their flashing red lights. No stranger would be able to get far.

The sky was turning dark and stormy. Hannah and Lila made it to the west entrance. A young deputy there was talking to Guthrie. Guthrie had his arms folded over his chest, his face drawn into somber lines. She waved. He nodded.

Hunter, where did you go?

Then Hannah heard calling in the distance, happy shouting. "They found the little boy!" "He's been found!" With Lila huffing beside her, she ran toward the voices.

Beaming, Aunt Ida and Aunt Edith waited several yards away from the corn dog stand. Hunter stood between them, their arms around his small trembling shoulders. The little boy clutched their skirts in his small fists.

With a shout of joy, Lynda rushed to him and swung him up in her arms. The crowd fell silent. Needing to be close, Hannah pushed her way forward.

"I'm sorry, Mommy!" Hunter sobbed. "I'm sorry. I didn't mean to get losted."

Billy and Guthrie came into view, running from opposite directions. The crowd parted to let them and the sheriff and a deputy through.

Billy cried out, "Thank God! Where was he?"

Weeping, Lynda reached out her free arm, and the

two of them embraced each other with Hunter in the middle.

Guthrie halted a few paces back, though he looked like he wanted to snatch the child from their arms and hold him close.

Choked with emotion, Hannah made her way to Guthrie and took his arm. Emotions ran high, and she feared he might do or say something in the heat of the moment that would do harm. But he didn't pull against her. Instead, he closed his large hand over hers.

She tried to read his emotions, but she only had his profile to judge.

"Where were you, baby?" Lynda asked her son.

"I wanted...a corn dog." Hunter sniffed back tears.

"Yes?" Lynda prompted.

Hannah leaned her head against Guthrie's arm, suddenly feeling weak with relief.

"But then I saw a quarter under there." He pointed to a long, green-draped table across the way. "And I crawled over there. Then I saw a grasshopper and I wanted to catch him, but I couldn't. Then I came back out and I couldn't see Daddy and I got scared. So I hid under the table until my daddy came back to find me. I was scared some stranger would get me. I wanted my daddy."

Hannah blinked back tears. Happy endings were so rare.

Lynda and Billy hugged their son again.

"It's okay." Billy smoothed the little boy's hair. "We just wanted you to be safe."

Again, Hannah expected Guthrie to speak up. Again, he remained silent, watching. She squeezed Guthrie's arm reassuringly.

He returned the pressure.

Hannah smiled, Guthrie's silence bolstering her.

"Aunt Ida and Edith, how did you find him?" Lynda asked the beaming ladies.

"We just thought like a child," Ida replied.

"Absolutely. We know that strangers do abduct children nowadays." Edith frowned. "So the pastor had to call the sheriff and such—"

"But children do just wander away. Always have. I remember Guthrie doing it at this fair when he was about six." Ida glanced at her nephew. "We found him the same way. Looking where a child might hide."

"Well, no harm done." Hannah's father spoke. "Thank you, Sheriff. Sorry we called you out."

"No problem. You did just what you should. I was close by, and my two deputies were on-site and were able to close off the exits. If this had been an abduction, your quick action would have prevented him from getting away." He turned to the crowd. "Everyone, the excitement's over. It could rain any time, so let's have fun!"

Hoping no one had noticed her clinging to Guthrie, Hannah dropped her hold on his arm. People drifted away as the wind brought the rain.

Guthrie turned to her. "I'm beat. I'm heading home." His voice rasped with emotion.

"Me, too. Too much pie," Hannah agreed, tired, but with a heart full of thankfulness.

She didn't want Guthrie to be alone right now. Billy's losing Hunter might have rocked the new equilibrium of Guthrie trying to get along with his errant brother-in-law. Guthrie hadn't reacted with anger or recriminations, as she'd feared. She wanted to know why. "I'll leave my car for my parents. Can I have a ride home with you?"

He nodded and soon held the door open for her to climb into his truck. As he drove onto the highway, the rain, which had been holding off all day, finally began. A rhythmic pitter-patter over their heads gave Hannah a melancholy feeling. Guthrie appeared to drive on autopilot, not really aware of her presence.

Finally, she drew in a deep breath. "Thanks for not going ballistic over Hunter being lost."

"I wanted to."

She heard both the grudge and the honesty in his voice. "I know you did. That's why I'm thanking you for not making things worse than they were."

"Kids wander off."

"They do." She couldn't believe her ears. He wasn't blaming Billy!

"I could see that Billy was really terrified when he thought he'd lost Hunter." He spoke the words as if they'd been and still were a revelation to him.

"Yes, I'm glad you saw that." Inwardly, she rejoiced for Guthrie's change of heart. A major breakthrough.

She ventured on, choosing her words with care. "Billy is good with the kids. I think he's learning to be a father more each time he's with them. You have to remember he didn't have a father and he hasn't had the years of experience you've had with the kids."

Guthrie nodded, but distractedly, as though his mind was filled to the brim with conflicting thoughts.

She let him wrestle with switching his mind-set against his brother-in-law to acceptance that Billy had become a new man. She stared at the gray scene beyond the windshield. The steady rain infused her with a feeling that the two of them in the truck cab were cut off from the rest of the world. Maybe Guthrie had the same feeling.

Finally, he spoke up. "I saw how Lynda turned to Billy when Hunter came up missing. I think she's starting to have feelings for him again."

"I think she's learning to," Hannah replied haltingly. "Billy's not the only one who's changed, you know. I don't think Lynda is the same woman she was at seventeen when Billy married her."

"How do you mean that?"

"Well, life changes all of us." She propped her elbow by the passenger window and set her chin on her hand. "I've gone through something similar." She cleared her throat. "Until recently, I was engaged."

"You were?"

She nodded.

"Can you... Do you mind...?"

"No, I don't mind. I was engaged to Edward for three years. We attended the same college, and he gave me a ring our senior year."

Guthrie looked surprised as he drove into the yard between his house and the barn and parked. The rain thundered overhead. Neither of them moved to venture outside the truck.

"What happened?" he asked.

She felt a freedom blossoming inside her. She'd wanted to put her thinking about Edward into words for weeks. But in Petite, she hadn't had anyone she'd wanted to confide in—except this man. She hadn't realized that until right now. She wanted to tell Guthrie. She hoped he'd understand. "I don't think either of us was seeing clearly or had become our real selves, our adult selves, yet."

"What do you mean?"

"I wasn't really acting like myself." She looked into his face. "In fact, I didn't really know myself yet. I didn't realize it at the time. I was so caught up in wanting to be a pastor's wife like my mother that I'd assumed a persona that didn't fit me, and I agreed to marry a man I wasn't deeply in love with."

"You weren't in love with him?"

She shook her head. "Not deeply. Not till-death-do-us-part deep. I must have thought he was just like my father. You see, I wanted to marry someone good and wise like Dad."

"Your fiancé wasn't good and wise?"

"No, or maybe I shouldn't say that. But just because he wanted to be a pastor didn't mean he was just like my father. And it was wrong of me to expect him, anyone, to be. But it wasn't just Edward.

"*I've* changed so much since I finally faced the truth about how wrong my assumptions were. I think I was only a shadow of myself. Breaking out of a mousy self-image, coming here to Petite, taking on the challenge of working with you, I feel like a totally different woman." Speaking these words liberated her as if wind lifted her wings and she was flying.

Guthrie nodded. He tried to imagine Hannah's fiancé. What man would be willing to give up an interesting and warmhearted woman like Hannah?

"I think Edward realized something was wrong long before I did. I hung on until it was painfully obvious that it wasn't going to work out with us. Breaking the engagement hurt." She inhaled deeply and smiled at him. "Now I'm glad I broke it off. I just wish he'd said something earlier instead of letting it drag out for nearly three years."

"Maybe he didn't think it was right for a man to beg off."

Her eyes serious, she pursed her lips and nodded. "You're probably right. But then I discovered…"

"You don't have to tell me."

She twisted on the seat to face him and inched closer. "I want to…if you don't mind listening."

"I'd be honored." His throat thickened.

She stared at the window beyond Guthrie's head, then made eye contact with him. "Two months after I broke up with Edward, he married someone else."

"Two months?" He was incredulous. "He—he was…"

She nodded, obviously in pain. "He must have been seeing her. That's what hurts."

"It would."

"Even if Edward hadn't been dating her, he must have known that he had feelings for her, not me."

Guthrie couldn't speak. His throat had closed up. He reached over and pulled her to him. He wanted to comfort her. But the feeling of her softness in his arms went to his head. *Hannah, Hannah…*

He kissed her hair, fragrant with spices, then her eyebrows. Her eyes closed. He kissed her eyelids, first one, then the other. Petal soft. He rubbed her fine hair between his fingers. Such softness brought feelings, emotions bubbling up from deep inside him.

A warmth, healing and vital, flowed through him like a cleansing prayer. Bill and Lynda…it could work out. Maybe *he* might get a second chance, too. The words, "I love you" whispered through his mind. If he could be sure these words were true, would he be able to say them to this woman? Did he, had he fallen in love with Hannah?

Unsure of himself, Guthrie brushed his lips against hers. "Hannah, you make me believe anything is possible. You make me believe…."

Tilting her chin, Hannah smoothed his golden hair, then rested her hand on his cheek.

The gentle touch of her fingertips rushed through him like brushfire. "Hannah, you're a wonderful woman."

The words were spoken so softly that Hannah barely heard them. She was more aware of the bristly texture of Guthrie's jawline under her palm, his latent strength that made her feel safe and protected within his arms. Guthrie would never say "I love you" unless it were God's honest truth. He wouldn't fall in love with someone while another woman wore his diamond.

Hannah pressed her lips to Guthrie's. She wished she had the audacity to say those three words, "I love you," to him. Inside her head, they sounded so right. But if he didn't return her feelings, they could cost her this brand-new intimacy with this special man, this wonderful man. While gazing into his blue, blue eyes, she stroked his rough cheek, and sparks danced up her arm.

"I mean…Hannah, you're so special." He glanced down. "You've become a friend, more than a friend. Tonight when I could have caused trouble, you came close to me. Just your touch on my arm gave me the patience to see the bigger picture, give Billy another chance, give myself another chance."

His last phrase, barely audible, took her breath away. She drew closer still. "Guthrie, I—"

They paused, their faces only inches apart. Hannah remembered the sensation of his lips caressing hers. *Guthrie, kiss me again.*

The sound of a vehicle. Her parents drove up beside them in her SUV. Instinctively Hannah pulled away and waved to them. Disappointment swallowed her up as if she were entering a dark tunnel. She didn't know what she had made Guthrie believe, what second chance he referred to. But another moment alone and she could have found out!

Rain beat against the roof of her parents' nearly finished house. Hannah grunted with exertion as Guthrie hammered the final nail into the four-foot by eight-foot piece of wallboard they were holding in place.

"Well, that's the first bedroom done." Guthrie stepped back.

Hannah heaved a sigh and pulled off her work gloves. "Let's take a coffee break." She walked down the framed-in hallway to the kitchen with the speckled white counter they'd put in together.

Two days had passed since the evening they'd kissed. That evening, tensions between them over working together and over Billy and Lynda reconciling had ended. Since then, Guthrie had been quieter than usual.

This hadn't surprised her. Guthrie struck her as the kind of man who thought matters over very carefully before making a decision. She respected this, but she'd like a hint of what he was mulling over. Was he thinking of her as she was of him? Was he thinking of kissing her again?

Maybe a friendly cup of coffee would loosen his tongue. Hopeful, she drew out the glass coffeepot from the warmer and held it up in question.

"Sure. I'll have a cup. Heavy on—"

She took over with a grin. "Heavy on the cream—"

"And don't forget a teaspoon of sugar for you, not me," he finished for her.

She chuckled. "I think we've eaten too many breakfasts together." In fact, the opposite was true. She looked forward to their quiet times together at the breakfast table each morning. She even woke early to lengthen their time alone at the table while her parents slept late upstairs. She stirred his cup and handed it to him. "We no longer have any mystery left."

"That's not true. There's a lot I'd like to know about you."

About to take her first sip, she lifted her eyebrows. This sudden move into a more personal exchange heightened her awareness of him standing only a few feet away. "Like what?"

He slid onto a step stool. "Like what your plans are once this house is done."

Stumped, she leaned against the kitchen counter. How could she answer that question? She couldn't say the truth—*I'd like to stay with you at your house.* That might be what a twenty-first-century woman would say, but not this twenty-first century woman! She was looking for a lifelong mate. Was Guthrie? After all, they'd only shared a kiss—all right, two if you counted the one she'd surprised him with in the church attic.

Also she'd just broken a three-year engagement, and Guthrie was right in the midst of a family crisis.

And they'd only known each other two months! Recent events had already proved she'd made a poor decision when she'd accepted Edward's ring. Guthrie attracted her, but there just hadn't been enough time to gauge where all this was leading. She gave Guthrie the only honest answer she could. "I haven't decided."

"I'd like you to stay."

Hannah's heart did a quick double beat. She licked her dry lips. "You would?"

"I can't imagine Petite without you."

"Thanks. It's begun to feel like home to me, too."

"I'm glad."

But Hannah needed to know if Guthrie had done more than just think about reconciling with Billy. She didn't want the angry Guthrie to come back. She took her courage in her hands. "Have you talked to Lynda about Billy?"

"Yes, we had a long talk last night. Billy really sounds like he's changed for the better." He rose and set his empty mug on the counter. "Let's see if we can get two more rooms done today."

Though surprised, she followed suit. She had no choice. So much for sharing. *Guthrie, next please talk to Billy. With that resolved, then maybe we can talk about us, if there is a possibility for us.*

At the end of the long, exhausting day and during a pause in the pouring rain, Guthrie helped Hannah into his truck and drove them home. He parked beside the barn.

An unfamiliar sedan was parked close to his back porch.

"Whose car is that?" she asked tiredly, tightening and flexing her stressed shoulder muscles trying to relax them.

A stranger stepped out the back door and under the shelter of the little porch roof and stood there, waiting for them. The handsome man was dark-haired, tall and slender, dressed in expensive-looking gray chinos and a black sport shirt.

Guthrie made a sound of surprise. Hannah glanced at him. What about this stranger had startled him?

Guthrie got out of the truck. Unmindful of the lazy rain, which still sprinkled down, he opened her door, then led her to the porch. Though he didn't seem to hurry, Hannah sensed a tension in him.

"Brandon." Guthrie's tone was a puzzle to Hannah. Was it a greeting, a question, a challenge? She couldn't tell.

"Guthrie." The man responded in kind.

The warm sprinkle of rain refreshed Hannah, but the unspoken tension between the two men puzzled her. Guthrie hadn't been pleased to hear his brother was coming, and he certainly didn't sound welcoming now. What was wrong?

She offered her hand.

Guthrie said belatedly, "Hannah, this is my brother, Brandon."

Brandon walked down the steps and shook her hand.

As she exchanged pleasantries with Brandon, she

wondered about Guthrie's renewed quietness. She'd thought, over the afternoon, that he'd begun to loosen up again.

"Have you seen Lynda?" Hannah asked.

"No, but I'm looking forward to it and seeing the kids." Brandon looked at Guthrie. "Mom says Billy's back."

Guthrie nodded. "Yes, he's grown up a lot. He's great with the kids."

Hannah frowned at Guthrie's dead tone. *Something's dreadfully wrong here, Lord. What is it?*

"I'm glad." Brandon looked both uneasy and upset. "Which room do you want me to take?"

"I'm sorry," Guthrie replied. "I've already got Hannah and her parents living with me after a fire in town. Aunt Ida and Edith are expecting you to stay with them. I'll call them and tell them you're on your way in."

"No problem." Guthrie's brother reached inside the door, brought out a gray duffel and a suit bag and walked toward the sedan.

Hannah called after him, "I'm sorry. I could go to stay with the aunts."

"No, this is fine." With a wave, he got into his car and drove away.

She and Guthrie stayed where they were, then she rested a hand on his arm. "What is it?" she whispered.

He glanced at her. "Do you get the feeling everything's getting dumped here all at once? When Dad died, when we really needed him, Brandon couldn't be bothered. And now he's back. I don't get it.''

Hannah leaned close to him, resting her head on his arm. ''Oh, Guthrie, you dear man.'' First Billy, now Brandon.

''I don't know how to handle this. I feel like having it out with him, but what good would it do now? It wouldn't change anything.''

Hannah listened sympathetically but detected more in Guthrie's attitude toward Brandon. There was something else, some other unsettled business between these two brothers. *God, why does Guthrie have to deal with this right now? He just got adjusted to Billy coming back. Now Brandon shows up. I know You always know best, but couldn't this have waited?*

People crowded around Hannah in the brightly lit church basement to celebrate the new roof and refurbished attic. A large sheet cake was being slowly but surely devoured not only by the church members but by the good people of Petite. The marble cake with white icing bore the pink frosting salutation, Thanks Guthrie and Hannah!

Hannah shifted her weight on her tired feet and tried to ignore her uneasiness. Guthrie sat across the room with Hunter on his lap and talked with Ted and Billy. While Guthrie and Billy appeared to be making progress toward reconciliation, the unmentioned friction between Guthrie and Brandon had increased over the past few days.

Whenever Guthrie and Brandon were together,

Hannah noted others watching them, measuring them. Obviously, the town of Petite wasn't in the dark about the root of the distance between the two brothers. She wished someone would give her a hint. Though Guthrie put on a good face, she hurt for him, even though she knew the last thing he wanted was sympathy.

Standing at Hannah's side, Brandon and his mother sipped coffee with Lila. Martha ran her fingers through her damp hair. Everyone had been rained on as they rushed between car and church. "When will this rain stop? I'm so worried for the farmers. They need to be harvesting the corn and soybeans now. How will they ever get into these wet fields with their combines or get the corn dried out?"

"It's delaying the work on my café. I can tell you that," Lila added. "If it weren't for my insurance, I'd be sunk."

"I'm sorry to hear that, Lila," Brandon said. "I had been looking forward to stopping in the Cozy for a fried-egg sandwich."

"Well, you come over to my house and I'll fix you one." Lila patted his arm. "I wouldn't want to send you back to San Francisco without one!"

Brandon smiled.

But Hannah thought his smile looked brittle and his eyes forlorn. She sensed Brandon had come home for some specific reason. What was it?

"Hannah, if you and Guthrie hadn't gotten this roof done, who knows how much damage this rain would have caused." Lila looked at the ceiling as though assessing the destructive power of the rain beating against the basement windows.

Martha shook her head. "The ground was saturated already after the spring rains. Where will all this water go?"

Hannah had heard Martha's worry repeated over and over in the past week of solid rain. The Wisconsin River and its creeks were already full, and the subsoil was soaked. In the spring, flooding had been narrowly avoided, but now the threat had returned fourfold.

"There was no need to thank Guthrie and me. We were just glad to get the roof done." Hannah was becoming a little embarrassed. After all, she'd helped Guthrie with the roof for a selfish reason, to free him up to work on her parents' home.

"Looking at you, I can't believe you're a carpenter." Brandon gave her a quizzical look.

Hannah shrugged. *Brandon, I haven't figured you out yet myself.*

"Mom showed me the videotapes she had of you and my great-aunts," Brandon continued. "They are hilarious."

She smiled, but wearily. This type of comment was also wearing on her. Yes, the taped cooking spots were amusing, but that didn't diminish the quality of the recipes or the spontaneity the two aunts added to them. Hannah was proud of the recipes and the aunts. Her agent had called a day ago to say that the dairy wanted to continue to sponsor the spots after the first three-month contract and were talking about doing a promotional brochure booklet with dairy recipes. If that came about, her agent thought that demos might be picked up by Minneapolis and Milwaukee TV stations, too.

"I'm very grateful to your aunts." Hannah raised her voice so others could hear. "They add sparkle and charm to the cooking demos. I am in *their* debt."

Martha nodded. "This town has always underestimated my husband's aunts. I'm so happy that these TV spots show what they can do." She looked at Brandon. "You'll be happy to know that Hannah insisted they be paid for their contribution to the project."

Brandon looked more surprised than happy. "That's wonderful." He gave Hannah another searching look.

Guthrie approached Hannah from behind. He touched her shoulder. "They want us to go up to the attic for a few pictures."

"All right," Hannah assented, "but these have to be the last. I'm not very enthusiastic about all this fuss."

Guthrie nodded to Lila and his mother but ignored Brandon.

"I think I'll come along," Brandon said with a note of challenge in his tone.

"Suit yourself." Guthrie led Hannah by the hand to the attic.

Once there, Hannah and Guthrie posed for the two ladies who kept the church scrapbook while Brandon looked on. Brandon's presence seemed to nettle Guthrie, whose expression became stormy. Then just the three of them, Guthrie, Hannah and Brandon, remained in the attic.

Gales of rain thrashed the roof. The intensity overhead matched the friction between the two brothers. Watching the conflict in their gazes and body language, Hannah feared this would be their big showdown. It seemed to her that they circled each other like wrestlers sizing each other up. She said a quick prayer for peace.

"So?" Brandon challenged Guthrie. "Go ahead. I know what you're thinking. Ask me."

Guthrie stared at his brother. "Where's Deirdre? Didn't she want to visit her family, too? You won't tell Mom why she didn't come with you. Her parents haven't invited you over for as much as a cup of coffee—"

"Deirdre left me."

Guthrie's expression changed to shock. "Why would she leave you? What did you do to her?"

Brandon gave a sound of disgust. "Me? She's the one who's filed for divorce. According to her, I'm not the man she thought I was when she married me. wasn't rising fast enough for her. So she found a man with big bucks who was looking for a trophy wife She decided his checkbook was just her size."

Guthrie took a step forward. "That can't be true Dee would never do something like that. She loved you."

Hannah listened in stunned silence as the two brothers evidently forgot her presence.

Brandon waved his hand dismissively. "You never knew the real Deirdre. I didn't wake up and realize how selfish she was till Dad died."

"Just because Dee isn't here to defend herself, I won't let you get away with saying things against her—"

Hannah wished she could disappear.

Brandon interrupted, "I should have known better than to fall for Deirdre! She drove a wedge between us from the beginning. I came back from school out east and thought you two had just dated. Why didn't you tell me what the depths of your feelings were for her? You still haven't forgiven me for marrying your first love, but you don't know how lucky you are. Did it ever occur to you that the reason I couldn't help Lynda or you out was that Deirdre spent every penny I made before I even brought the check home? Do you know how I felt when Dee told me she was leaving me? You couldn't guess. After four years with her, I felt nothing but relief!" Brandon turned away and hustled down the steps.

Guthrie headed after him. Hannah was right behind Guthrie. At the bottom, Brandon headed to the party, but Guthrie turned to the door. Hannah followed him. One second outside and chill rain soaked Hannah to her skin. Guthrie hurried ahead of her. By the dim light of the high pole lamp, she ran after him, slipping and stumbling on the wet gravel. He reached his truck and wrenched open the door. Sprinting, she closed the gap in time to throw open the passenger door as he cranked the key in the ignition.

"I'm going home!" he shouted over the noise of the rain pounding on the truck's roof.

"I'm coming, too!" She clambered inside and slammed the door behind her.

He clenched the steering wheel. "Stay here. I'm not going to be good company."

"You shouldn't be alone now." Brandon's words about marrying Guthrie's first love must be true. The thought made Hannah heartsick.

"I'm going to be alone the rest of my life." He glared at her. "I might as well accept that fact."

"Not if I have anything to say about it." Her words startled her, but she wouldn't take them back. It didn't have to mean anything more than one friend helping another. Even though she wanted so much more from Guthrie. Pushing away her own reaction to Brandon's news, she matched Guthrie's stare. Rain dripped from her hair and slid down the back of her neck.

He gunned the motor and took off.

Chapter Thirteen

Hannah had to hold on to the handgrip over the door as he sped down the road and out of town. The late September wind had picked up, and the rain could only be termed a deluge. The wipers battled in vain. She didn't know how Guthrie managed to stay on the road. The only explanation was that he knew the road well enough to navigate without seeing it.

She wished she'd brought her purse and cell phone with her. She hoped her parents wouldn't worry about her. But they would want her to stay with Guthrie and help him get over the shock of hearing that Deirdre had left Brandon for another man. After the breakup with Edward, Hannah knew how he must be feeling.

Guthrie slowed at an intersection.

Before Hannah could gasp, a low black car came out of nowhere—right across their path.

The truck fishtailed. Guthrie wrestled the steering

wheel. He pumped the brakes. The truck skidded to a halt, sliding onto the muddy shoulder.

He jerked it into park. ''Are you all right?''

''I'm fine.'' Hannah leaned her head back, the shock waves vibrating through her.

''Idiot!'' He hit the wheel with both hands. ''He could have killed someone!''

She nodded. *Us! He could have killed us! God, go with that driver and please keep him from hurting anyone, himself included.*

Guthrie threw open his door and climbed out.

Anxious to help, Hannah got out the passenger side, right into the muddy shoulder. Her sandals sunk into the mire up to her ankles.

Gripping the door, she hoisted herself onto the seat, composed herself, then lifted her feet outside into the shower. Within seconds, the mud had been rained off. She closed her door and crawled over to the other side and let herself out, her need to help Guthrie pushing her into the harsh elements. *God, guide Guthrie so he can see the truth about himself and his family. Help him to feel Your love for him.*

In the glow of the red rear lights, Guthrie was standing on the highway staring at his back passenger side wheel, buried in the muck up to the bottom of the wheel rim.

''Can you get it out?'' she shouted, shivering, her wet clothes clinging to her in the lashing wind.

''Yeah! I'm just disgusted with myself for getting stuck.''

That sounded more like the Guthrie she'd come to

know. Already his good humor and honesty were reasserting themselves. Thank Heaven! "It wasn't your fault! Anyone else wouldn't have been able to avoid a collision!"

He climbed up over the wheel well and into the truck bed. "Can you help?" He held a long wood plank over the side to her.

"Sure!" She accepted one, then another rough, wet plank and propped them against the side of the truck.

He climbed out and took one.

"What are you going to do?"

"I'll put these under the wheel, then drive onto them and out."

"Won't they just sink in the mud?" she asked. "I tried to get out the other side and sunk up to my ankles."

"It's all I've got!"

"Okay." She watched him work the planks under the mired wheel.

"Get in," he directed.

She hopped inside and slid across the seat. He climbed in and slowly gave the truck enough gas to ease them out of the mud. He parked on the road with his four-way flashers on, then retrieved his planks and threw them into the truck bed.

The rest of the way home he drove more carefully, and she started to relax in spite of her soaked clothing and concern for Guthrie. By the time they reached the farmhouse, she was shivering in earnest with the chill.

"You're going to catch a cold," he said gruffly.

"I'll be f-fine."

"I'm going to get you inside and into a hot shower."

She thought of arguing and then wondered why. This was the Guthrie she loved, the man who couldn't help caring for others. She grinned. "Sounds too good to be true."

He parked and hustled her through the unrelenting rain and in the back door. "Now run upstairs and shower. I'll put the kettle on for hot tea."

"Oh, please, I'd love some of that spiced cider your mom brought from the farmer's market, warmed up."

"I'll put it on now." He pushed her toward the staircase. "Take your time."

She paused. "I'll save you some hot water."

"Don't worry about me. I'm not cold. I'll just change into some dry clothes."

Hannah hurried through a steamy shower and into her new blue flannel pajamas and matching thick terry-cloth robe and slippers.

"Cider's hot," Guthrie called from the kitchen. "Your parents called and said they'd be home soon."

She scurried down the steps and into the warm kitchen, redolent with the fragrance of apples and cinnamon. "Mmm. That smells delicious." She sat down and accepted the daisy mug with a cinnamon stick in it. She held the cup between her hands and touched it to her cheek, then her forehead, enjoying the warmth it radiated. Her kitten, Sunny, hopped on her lap and began kneading a spot on the thick terry cloth for himself. Hannah enjoyed petting the soft fur, the cat's purring soothing her frazzled nerves.

Guthrie sat across from her, still looking upset.

Dear man. "Why don't you tell me about it? A trouble shared is a trouble halved."

He hung his head. "What do I need to tell you? You heard it all. No secrets left."

Impulsively, she reached over and took his hand. Her palm tingled with the contact. Edward's touch never overwhelmed her like this. "I told you about my engagement."

"I don't have any engagement to tell you about."

"Brandon said—"

"My brother said a lot, too much."

His dour mood had lifted, but traces lingered. She hated the fact that a woman had come between the brothers. Whether Brandon's words had been true or not, they'd upset Guthrie. She didn't know what to say, how to go on. She closed her eyes, asking for inspiration, then looking up, she asked, "Don't you trust me, Guthrie?"

At this, he met her gaze. "Sure."

"We've become friends, and friends don't dodge the truth."

"I guess so." He nodded.

"Did Brandon tell the truth? Did you love the girl he married?"

He slipped his hand from hers. "Yes."

Bereft of his touch, she waited, letting this one word really sink in. She shivered at what it meant. Guthrie had loved Deirdre. It explained so much, why

Guthrie hadn't married yet, why he hadn't been happy
to see his brother come home for a visit. Guthrie's
faithfulness was one of his most endearing traits, but
it could also work against him. Did he still have feelings for Deirdre? He hadn't given Hannah any hint
of it. Did she have a chance with this man?

Still stroking the silky kitten, she began slowly. "I
thought I was in love with Edward. Maybe you
thought you were in love with Deirdre. Perhaps if you
saw her now, you'd think a lot differently."

"I can't believe what Brandon said. Deirdre loved
him." He twisted halfway from her.

"But we all change. You're remembering a high
school girl." She longed to rise and walk around the
table. She wanted to cradle Guthrie's face in her two
hands and stroke his thick hair. He was such a dear
man. She'd never thought or felt this about Edward.
Why hadn't she noticed it at the time?

She forced herself to concentrate on the words he
needed to hear. "Even if Deirdre came back here, do
you think she'd still be the same girl you knew?"

He shrugged and propped his elbows on his thighs.
His chin rested on his fists. "I don't know what to
tell you. Everything's happened all at once."

"I don't know how you feel about me now. But I
thought the other evening after Hunter was found, you
and I came close to… I think we could become more
than friends, Guthrie. Or, at least, we have a chance
to go in that direction." She paused, her heart speeding up with uneasiness. She had to be honest, but she
couldn't take all the risks. Guthrie had to do his part.

He stared at the floor. "Dee and I dated on and off all through high school. She'd run hot, then cold, if you know what I mean." He glanced up.

Hannah nodded.

"After senior prom, I told her I loved her, but she didn't want to marry. She said she wasn't ready to settle down. I thought I'd just have to wait until she was ready."

Closing her eyes, Hannah imagined how Guthrie must have reasoned this out.

"Then I graduated from high school and Brandon came back after finishing law school. Mom and Dad had a party for us. The next thing I knew Dee and he were dating, then when he got a job offer in San Francisco, they eloped."

Hannah hated to be cynical, but everything Guthrie said made her believe Brandon's words at the church had been true.

"The only way I accepted Dee marrying Brandon was that she loved him more than she had cared for me. But now he tells me she didn't. How can I believe in love?"

Oh, Guthrie, you don't understand subterfuge, dishonesty or selfishness at all. Lord, give me the words, Your healing words.

Careful not to disturb the kitten napping on her lap, she took his hand. "You do believe in love. I don't think you realize what a loving man you are. You are a man filled with love for his family. That's love."

"That's not the kind of love I mean."

"Every kind of good love is related. Don't tell me

you don't believe in love when I see the love you have in action.''

He pulled his hand away and wouldn't meet her eyes.

''Guthrie, are you going to let all that you are, your strength of character, your kind heart, be turned inward, wasted? Or are you going to share it?''

He turned a somber gaze to her.

I love you, Guthrie! She imagined wrapping her arms around Guthrie and reveling in his warm, brawny embrace. ''You helped your sister when she really needed it. Not just with money, but with time and affection for her children. You've forgiven the man who hurt her and your father during his last days on earth. You carry a load of debt for Lynda and her children, yet you didn't charge the church a penny for the labor to fix the roof. You are a wonderful man.''

He pushed his fingers through his hair. ''I'm just a regular guy.''

She swallowed, gathering her courage. She had to shock him out of this blue funk. ''You have to use the same honesty with Brandon that you used with Billy.''

''What do you mean?''

''I mean when you saw how much Billy loved his kids, you began to give him a second chance.'' The kitten on her lap slept peacefully as she stroked its soft fur. The cat's blissful slumber contrasted with the wrenching emotion in Guthrie's voice. She centered herself in her love for Guthrie, her spirit of trust in God.

"How can I know if what Brandon has said is true?"

"Maybe that isn't what God's trying to get you to learn with Brandon."

"Well, what am I supposed to be learning?" Guthrie grumbled.

Hannah gathered her thoughts. "You changed toward Billy because you saw that he had changed, reformed. Maybe with Brandon, you need to show love to him whether he's right or not. God doesn't love us because we're good. He just loves us—no matter what."

Guthrie stilled, gazing into her eyes. "For while we were yet sinners, Christ died for us," he recited softly.

She nodded and replied with a companion verse. "We love Him because He first loved us."

He exhaled deeply. "I'll pray about it, but I'll need God's help to get over this...if I can get over this." He looked into her eyes. "Why do you put up with me, Hannah Kirkland?" He lifted her hand and kissed it.

Her heart thrummed in her ears.

"I'm sorry if I upset you tonight," Guthrie continued. "I wish we could go away somewhere and be together. There are so many things I've wanted to tell you, but here it's just one thing after another—"

The phone rang.

With a grimace, Guthrie picked up the receiver of the wall phone. "What? Don't worry. I'll come right in."

"What is it?" His expression had her worried.

"The creeks have overflowed their banks. My aunts need me."

Flood? She stood up, carefully letting the kitten jump down. "I'm coming with you."

"The river is expected to crest at Portage four feet above flood level in two days."

"What does that mean to Petite?" She imagined her parents' new house being washed away.

"The downtown near the bridge will be under water."

Lynda and the aunts' houses flooded! "Oh, no."

"The state is sending out sandbags. The Red Cross will be bringing in volunteers. I've got to get to town and start helping my family get ready."

"Wait for me. It'll only take me a minute to get into jeans and sweatshirt. Please write a note for my parents."

"I'm just going to my aunt's to move stuff from the basement to the attic. You don't—"

"*Please* wait for me." She raced for the stairs.

About three hours later, Hannah's hands quivered with exhaustion as she held a cup of decaf coffee.

"Guthrie, you and Hannah need to get some rest," Aunt Ida said as she poured cream into her own cup.

After hours of working silently beside Hannah and Guthrie, Brandon had refused coffee and had gone to bed.

Guthrie looked up. "We still need to move—"

"We're putting our foot down." Edith shook her

finger at him. "Now Ida is going to bunk in with me tonight. Hannah, you will take my bed—"

Hannah objected, "No, I—"

Ida wagged her finger at Hannah. "Don't argue. Guthrie can sleep on the couch in the parlor."

For the second time that night, Hannah found herself dressed for bed, this time in a borrowed lavender-flowered nightgown. Edith's room had been stripped of almost everything but the bed. Even the rose-patterned rug had been rolled up. Guthrie planned to store their beds and the sofa in Hannah's parents' unfinished home, which perched well above flood stage.

Bone-weary, Hannah sighed and lay down upon the bed. Moving furniture had been exhausting, but her earlier conversation with Guthrie about Brandon had taken its toll, too. The two brothers had worked side by side, but Brandon's bitter words had been too fresh for both of them to put aside. She'd seen them trying to cooperate, but the hurt was still there between them.

Fatigue weighed down her arms and legs. Her thoughts drifted. Dawn would come within a few short hours. Just as she closed her eyes, she heard Guthrie groan and collapse onto the sofa. So near and yet so far.

For a second, Hannah savored the memory of Guthrie's tender kisses. They had drawn her heart closer to him and evoked a longing for more. She took in a ragged breath.

Lord, help Guthrie learn to let the past go. Soften

*his heart toward his brother. I'm so tired.... Good
night. I mean, amen.*

Morning dawned, a rainy blustery morning. In her
Packer sweatshirt and jeans from last night, Hannah
stood in the aunts' kitchen talking on the phone to
Lynda. Around her, the two aunts were cooking a
substantial breakfast for them, scrambled eggs, bacon,
pancakes. The delightful fragrances made Hannah's
stomach do flip-flops of anticipation.

"What?" Hannah couldn't believe what Lynda had
just said.

"Bill has to leave this morning for a court appearance in Oneida County," Lynda repeated. "I'm going
with him."

"When will you be back?"

"He said we'll be back as soon as we can. He said
it could take more than one day."

"How serious is it?"

"It's a misdemeanor left over from his past. He's
hoping the judge will dismiss the charge in light of
the changes he's made in his life. He has a lawyer
hired and affidavits from his drug counselor and boss
in Chicago, his boss here and your father."

"You said we. He's letting you go with him?"

"Yes, I pestered him till he finally gave in. Mom
and the great-aunts will take care of the kids."

Hannah's heart sank. This development would hit
Guthrie when he was already down. "Okay. I'll be
praying for Billy."

"Don't worry, Hannah. I know Guthrie will be upset, but Bill couldn't put this off any longer."

Guthrie, followed by Brandon, entered the kitchen.

"Your sister wants to speak to you." Hannah handed him the phone.

"What is it, Lynda?" Guthrie asked gruffly.

Hannah sat at the table and gave him a tentative smile. This news on top of everything else gave new meaning to the phrase, "It never rains but it pours."

Guthrie listened with a worried look. "Do you have to go with him?" Pause. "Okay. We'll pray for you two." He hung up and sat across from her.

Brandon slid into the chair beside Hannah. "Good morning."

Hannah greeted him an uneasy smile.

"What's wrong?" Brandon glanced at her, then at his brother.

"More bad luck," Guthrie muttered. "Can't anything go right?"

"Now we'll have none of that at the breakfast table," Aunt Ida scolded from the stove where she was flipping pancakes. "A lot has gone right. We've got Hannah and her parents."

"And Bill's back," Edith added. "By the way, I think we should call him Bill now. He's grown up."

"That's right," Ida concurred. "And Brandon's home finally."

Guthrie's expression didn't lighten.

"Now cheer up, Guthrie," Ida urged.

Brandon nodded. "Yeah, you don't have any real problems. No one's divorcing you."

"Brandon, it wasn't right for you to take up with Deirdre right after she broke up with your brother." Ida shook her spatula at him.

"You wouldn't have liked it if he'd done that to you," Edith agreed. She was lifting bacon out of the cast iron frying pan onto paper toweling.

"And we knew that Deirdre only married you, Brandon, to get out of this town." Ida scooped the last of the griddle cakes onto a platter and brought them to the table.

Edith began cooking scrambled eggs. "The fact is she didn't love either of you."

"She's the kind of woman who never brings peace to a home, only strife." Ida poured everyone coffee and sat down.

The two men stared at their great-aunts, plainly not believing their ears.

Brandon recovered first. "I wish you'd told me all this nearly four years ago," he said with a sour twist to his mouth.

"Deirdre was what we used to call a siren. You wouldn't have listened to us four years ago." Edith put the platter of bacon and eggs on the table and sat down.

Ida nodded. "No, just like if we told Guthrie now that he'd better hold on to Hannah and not let her leave Petite, he wouldn't listen, either."

Hannah pursed her lips, but a giggle still slipped out of her mouth. Leave it to the aunts! "Thank you, ladies."

Guthrie started to speak, but was interrupted.

"Any time, dear." Ida patted Hannah's hand. "Edith, will you say the blessing?"

They all joined hands and Edith said, "Dear God, please give the young men and women who will be sandbagging today strength, good health and safety. Please give our nephews the faith and wisdom they need to end the strife in this family. Thank you, Lord, for everything, even this flooding. Amen."

The prayer touched Hannah's emotions. This was the prayer of the truly faithful, thanking God for everything, even the trials. She swallowed to keep back tears. Too little sleep and too much conflict were getting to her.

"Guthrie, don't frown so," Ida said gently. "Bill and Lynda will be back before we know it. And in the meantime you can concentrate on settling things with Brandon."

Hannah's eyes widened. The aunts' batteries were certainly charged today!

"I'm just supposed to forget my feelings?" Guthrie frowned. "I don't have any right to them, I suppose?"

"No, that's not what your aunt means," Hannah declared. "She just means life goes on. Bill deserted his family but has now changed. Your brother has discovered the truth about his wife and is going to have to go through a painful divorce—"

Ida cut in. "That's right, dear. Now, everyone, eat! Angry words upset digestion!"

Guthrie nodded. "I'll be fine. We've gotten through worse than this." He lifted his fork, but in spite of his brave words, his defeated expression hurt Hannah's heart. He looked like a man without hope. How could he entertain thoughts of a future they might share if he couldn't hope?

"Eat your breakfast, Guthrie." Aunt Ida frowned. "It will be a long hard day."

"Yes," Edith said, "after you finish moving Lynda's belongings up to the attic, you'll have a rough day or two of sandbagging. The state has started down by the bridge over the river by Lila's motel. The Red Cross is due by noon."

As if in response, the rain outside gushed harder. Hannah quivered at the thought of going back outside to be drenched again, but it couldn't be avoided. Whether Guthrie continued to reject the possibility of a happy ending for Brandon, Lynda or himself, the whole town of Petite faced a long hard fight to keep the water at bay.

Hannah closed her eyes for a moment. *Lord, Guthrie is a wonderful man, but please shake him out of this new slump, this dark valley we're in. Maybe it will never work out for us, but he needs help to accept Brandon back into his family. Please be with Bill and Lynda today as they try to put the past behind them once and for all. Soothe Brandon's broken heart. And lift Guthrie's spirits. Give him back his hope. I think I love him, Lord!*

Chapter Fourteen

Hannah had water in her boots and mud up her nose. In a line of about twenty-five volunteers, she and Guthrie worked side by side moving sandbags to reinforce the river levee. Guthrie handed her another soggy, sand-filled cloth bag. Her arms had the strength of overcooked spaghetti. Shivering in the cold rain, she nearly dropped it, but managed with a grunt to heft it on to the next person. Since morning light they'd lifted a mountain of bags to create a wall to protect Petite from the waters of the Wisconsin River, their only hope to keep Petite from flooding.

Without warning, Hannah's knees buckled. She sank down in the soupy mud that surrounded them. The steady rain and cold gusts beat against her hooded yellow rain slicker. Her heart raced, and she breathed rapidly as if she'd been running. *We still have more bags to put into place!*

"What's wrong?" Guthrie asked.

"I can't get up." She felt like a flattened toothpaste tube—all her stuff had been used up. She knew she should feel something about this. But a pervasive numbness tamped down everything except the sensations of being exhausted and cold to the bone.

A man wearing a Red Cross vest ran down the line tapping shoulders. "Come on. A group of students from Madison has come to relieve you. The Red Cross van has hot coffee and sandwiches. And there are blankets and cots at the church. You've done a great job! Now move out and make room for the fresh workers."

Catching her hands, Guthrie pulled Hannah to her feet. She leaned against him as he half-carried her up the levee. Without his support, she knew she would be crawling on her belly up the muddy incline.

"Guthrie!" a familiar voice called. "Hannah?"

Hannah looked up to find her sister right in front of her. "Doree!" Shock. Joy. She threw her arms around her sister's slender shoulders. "Why? What…"

"I came as soon as I heard the announcement on the TV asking for volunteers. How are Mom and Dad?"

Hannah found herself weeping.

Wearing a red vinyl poncho like a beacon in the gray scene, Doree put one hand on each side of Hannah's face. "Hannah, what's wrong! Did something happen to—"

"She's just overtired." Guthrie reclaimed Hannah so she could lean against him again. "We've been tossing around furniture and sandbags since breakfast.''

"Mom and Dad are fine." Hannah tried to smile. "They're coordinating with the Red Cross at the church. I'm fine. If only this rain would stop."

"I've got to go now. Tell them I'll see them later." Doree walked backward, still talking. "I'll talk with you later!"

Hannah nodded as Guthrie led her away. She looked up and gave him a weak smile.

"Don't worry." Guthrie tucked her closer. "We're going to the Red Cross van. We'll pick up some food, then head for the church to sleep."

Soon he sat her in a chair in the warm church basement. A plate of sandwiches sat on her lap. She couldn't remember carrying them.

"Eat," Guthrie ordered.

She stared at the food, unable to pick up a sandwich. "I...can't."

"Here." He lifted a cup of coffee to her lips. "Careful. It's hot. Just sip it."

Strong hot coffee trickled inside her, warming as it went. "I'm so cold."

"That wind made us feel the chill more." He held a sandwich to her lips. "Eat."

She opened her mouth, bit and chewed. "I'll try to feed myself." She couldn't remember that chewing had ever been such hard work before. Her taste buds seemed to be out of order, too. She only felt the texture of bread on her tongue. She glanced at Guthrie.

He looked as though eating had become a chore for him, also. "You need to eat, too."

"I don't need any encouragement." He devoured a sandwich in two bites and picked up another. With his other hand, he put her sandwich to her lips. "Come on. A few more bites and you'll get enough strength to finish your meal."

"Okay." She chewed and swallowed another bite. Tuna fish, the sandwich was tuna fish.

With a groan, Brandon collapsed onto the chair next to them. "Whew. My muscles are getting muscles."

She stared at him. Her tired brain reminded her Brandon and Guthrie were at odds, but she couldn't manage to act as a buffer between them right now. She needed to focus all her energy on taking her sandwich from Guthrie's hand and lifting it to her mouth.

"I'm surprised you've held up, big brother," Guthrie said in a calm voice, then devoured another sandwich.

Hannah concentrated on chewing. Guthrie was right. The food and coffee were bringing her back.

"I'm not the weakling you may think I am." Brandon swallowed half a sandwich. "I work out regularly. But I am tired."

"So am I," Guthrie said.

"Wow." Brandon's eyebrows shot up. "I'm surprised to hear you admit that."

"Don't fuss," Hannah mumbled. Finishing her sandwich and coffee, she handed the plate and cup to Brandon. The food had made her feel human again, but her exhaustion couldn't wait. "I can't sit up anymore. I've got to lie down."

Handing his plate to his brother, Guthrie jumped up and led her to cots that had been set up in the Sunday school rooms. She lay down on the first empty one and fell asleep instantly.

Guthrie gazed at her, warm emotions surging through him. Hannah. She'd worked beside him last night and all day, helping out the town she'd only lived in for a couple of months. She'd worked as hard as any of them. She'd become a part of them already. What a woman!

Bending over her, he pulled off her boots, which stuck out over the end of the cot, and opened her slicker. "Take a break, Hannah. You deserve it." The temptation to kiss her lured him. Her soft lips invited his touch, but he'd been such a jerk lately. What had gotten into him, grumbling at everyone? At Hannah. She'd talked to him straight, spoken the truth. His bruised heart felt a touch of warmth, healing.

"She's really something, you know that?" Brandon appeared at his elbow.

Guthrie kept his gaze on Hannah's face. "Yes, she's a real lady."

"Don't let her get away." Brandon turned.

Guthrie caught his brother's elbow. "I'm...I'm glad...."

Brandon glanced over his shoulder. "I'm glad I'm here this time, too. Will you give me another chance?"

Guthrie thought a second, picking out his words

with care. "Our family always gives a second chance."

Brandon blinked back tears and walked away quickly.

Guthrie stared at Hannah. *Will you give me a second chance? I've let my family, my anger get in the way.* Would she give him the right to kiss her, to love her?

"Hannah! Hannah!"

Hannah opened her eyes and stared at the strange ceiling. *Where am I?*

"Hannah!"

Small hands tugged at her shoulder.

She glanced into Amber's face. "What is it?"

"Misty's not in the church. She's lost."

Hannah's mind tried to process the sentence. Couldn't.

"Our kitty's lost!" Jenna shouted from the other side of Hannah. "Help us!"

Hannah sat up. "When did you find that she was lost?"

Amber looked near tears. "We were playing with her, but she wanted to go outside—"

Jenna cut in. "Mommy told us not to go outside. But we didn't have a cat box."

Amber took over again. "So we let Misty outside. But she didn't come back!"

"Where's your mother?" Hannah stretched, trying to wake up her stiff and aching body. She slid her feet into her soggy rubber boots.

"She's outside helping put up the sandbags so the water doesn't get us," Jenna replied.

"But we don't want the water to get Misty, either." Amber's teary eyes were as round as dimes.

Hannah stood up, tugging her yellow slicker around her. If she didn't take care of this, the children would disturb someone else or try to find the cat themselves and probably get lost or worse. "Okay."

"You'll take us to find her?"

"No, you girls must stay here inside where it's warm and dry. Who's taking care of you?"

"The great-aunts." Amber took Hannah's hand.

"Take me to them."

Through the darkened church basement, where volunteers slept on cots and floor, the girls led her to the church kitchen. Both the aunts lay, curled up in blankets, sleeping on the benches on each side of the built-in table. In the low light, Hannah looked at the kitchen clock that read five forty-seven. Barely sunup. She sighed.

"Don't disturb your aunts. Come to the front door with me." The side entrance had been sandbagged shut, along with the whole foundation of the church, to keep water out. This precaution had been taken even though the church sat on a rise above most of Petite.

Upstairs, Hannah opened the double church doors. A gray dawn met her gaze. The chill rain poured down like a constant running faucet. The sound irritated her. Why couldn't it just stop?

"We'll come out with you," Jenna offered.

"No! Don't you dare step a foot outside. If you do, I'll come right back in." Hannah fastened her slicker and pulled a small flashlight from her pocket. "Now go sit by a window and watch me."

The little girls turned away, and Hannah closed the door firmly behind her. She walked down the rain-slick steps. Rain splashed into her face. Wind whistled through the leaves above, giving the wind a voice. Shouting echoed in the distance, farther up the shoreline. The crew had made progress building the barrier against the rising water. The flood crest should come in a few hours. Either the sandbags would hold the water at bay, or they wouldn't.

Hannah knew she'd have to return to the sandbagging after breakfast. The all-night crew would be ready to be replaced. Doree was out there in the shadowy predawn. Mom and Dad had probably gone to Guthrie's for a few hours of sleep. Her little kitty, Sunny, probably slept at the end of their bed.

"Misty. Misty," she called in a high, sweet cat-calling tone. "Here kitty, kitty." She stumbled through the muddy parking lot, filled with familiar and unfamiliar vehicles. She bent over, looking underneath them, thinking the cat might be hiding under one.

She dragged herself down one aisle of mud-splashed vehicles, then another until she came to the north edge of the lot. "Misty, here kitty."

"Me…eee…uuuu," a little feline voice pleaded. "Me…eee…uuuu."

Hannah looked up to see the drenched kitten halfway up an old oak tree at the edge of the church cemetery just beyond the parking lot. Some noise, some stray dog must have frightened the kitten into scampering high. Well, the kitten hadn't gotten very far up, and the tree wasn't too high or hard to climb. She could rescue Misty. She waved at the church windows and pointed toward the cat. She wanted the girls to know she'd found their kitten.

She took hold of the lowest branch and tried to walk her feet up the gnarled trunk. Her feet slid down. She dropped her hold and shook off her boots and tried again in her socks. She needed to grip the tree with her feet. This time she made it and swung herself up and around to sit on the branch, which swayed with her weight. "Come on," she murmured to the tree, "I'm not that heavy."

Reaching up, she grasped the next branch and stood, then hoisted herself onto the branch where Misty crouched.

"Hold on, Misty." Hannah sat on the branch. "I'll get you." She continued to talk to the kitten to keep the little creature from being frightened into climbing higher. "Come here, Misty. Here, kitty, kitty."

Soaked to her skin and trembling with the cold, Misty mewled more plaintively than ever. The frightened kitten didn't budge.

"Oh, dear." Hannah sighed. She inched out on the branch slowly, slowly, then caught the kitten with the tips of her fingers and dragged it to her. The limb beneath them swayed. Cradling the kitten close to her, she made comforting sounds to Misty.

Ever so carefully, Hannah shoved herself in reverse until her back touched the trunk of the tree. Her heart pounded in her ears. Her weariness had sapped her reserve energy. She leaned against the trunk and hoped for a spurt of energy. And how could she get down one-handed?

"Hannah." Guthrie's unexpected voice came from below her. "Can you get down?"

"No, I don't think I can. I just have no energy, and the branches are so slippery. I'm afraid I'll drop the kitten." Her words tumbled out one on top of the other.

"Wait there. I'll get my truck."

Hannah couldn't figure out what the truck could do for a cat in a tree, but her mind was too fuzzy to think. Within minutes, she heard the truck park underneath her.

"Okay, Hannah, look at me."

She glanced down at Guthrie, who was standing in his truck bed right beneath her.

"Now lean forward, wrap one arm around the branch in front of you and hand Misty down to me."

Hannah obeyed. Her fingertips held the kitten about two feet above Guthrie's hands.

"Just drop her. I'll catch her."

She let go of the kitten and Guthrie caught it.

"Now wrap both arms around the branch and let your feet down. Then I'll be able to get hold of you."

Again she followed directions. Just as her hold on the limb slipped way, she found herself sliding into

Guthrie's brawny arms. She tucked her chin against his neck and rested on his strength. *Safe.*

"Oh, Hannah," Guthrie murmured. "Only you would climb a tree in the middle of a deluge to rescue a kitten, even if you are exhausted and even if you didn't know how you could get down. You wonderful, crazy, hardheaded woman!" He hugged her.

"I've been an idiot getting mad and not paying you the attention I should. You're right—whatever happened to Bill and Lynda, what does that mean to us? So Deirdre didn't love me or my brother. What does this have to do with us? Have I ruined everything we could have between us, getting stuck in the past, holding onto the pain? I love you, Hannah. I see that now, and nothing will ever change it. You sweet, loving woman." He kissed her. Again. Again. "Hannah, my sweet Hannah."

Clinging to his shoulders, Hannah gave herself up to the bountiful sensations and deep emotions stirred by kissing Guthrie. *This man is the one, Lord! I see it, feel it so clearly now!* She couldn't stop kissing him. "I love you, too, you stubborn, irritating, wonderful man."

Rain flowed over their heads like a shower of blessing, a baptism of love. Hannah clung to Guthrie. His warmth joined with hers overcame the nip of the dawn. Holding him and being held by him struck Hannah as the most wonderful gift she'd ever received.

"Guthrie! Guthrie!" Aunt Ida scolded from the church doorway. "Bring Hannah and Misty in right now. You can finish kissing Hannah and proposing to her inside the church.''

"Yes, you don't want your bride to catch her death of cold!" Edith admonished.

Guthrie looked at Hannah with a grin. "Will you?"

She gazed into his blue, blue eyes, knowing that this was his proposal, honest and direct, just like the man. "I will, with all my heart." On the outside, she was rain-soaked and bone tired. Inside, her heart glowed with her love for Guthrie and the knowledge that he loved her, too, with a down-to-earth, till-death-do-us-part love. *Praise God from whom all blessings flow!*

Hannah and Guthrie stopped to smile at each other. They'd finished painting the last wall of her parents' new home. Outside the bay window, the first lazy snowflakes of winter floated down.

Guthrie reached over and dabbed his paintbrush, wet with light blue paint, on her nose.

"Don't start," Hannah warned him, waving her brush provocatively.

His brush held high, he pulled her to him and kissed her.

Hannah savored the spiral of warmth that curled through her. "I love you," she whispered against his lips.

"I love you, too, blue nose." He tightened his embrace. "Are you sure we have to wait till May to get married?"

"Hey, watch that stuff!" Lynda called as she walked inside. "It's addictive!"

"Too late! We're already hooked." Hannah smiled, but didn't leave Guthrie's luxurious embrace. With her free hand, she laid her brush across the paint can, and so did Guthrie.

"Just came to say goodbye," Bill said, entering after his wife. "I'm off to basic training."

Reluctantly abandoning her fiancé's arms, Hannah went over and hugged Bill. "We'll miss you."

"But you're doing the right thing." Smiling, Guthrie shook Bill's hand.

Hannah rejoiced at the sight.

Bill's court date, which had taken him away during the flooding, had ended in a dismissal of all charges. With his slate clean, Bill had enlisted in the army, and his future with Lynda and the children was plotted out.

After basic training, his family would accompany him for four years of military duty, after which Bill intended to enroll in college full-time for a career in counseling. Hannah always felt a little teary when she thought of Bill and Lynda's reunion. And the mountain of sandbags they'd put up had protected Petite. The future looked bright for the small town. Praise God, everything had turned out well.

"This house is going to be just lovely." Lynda looked around with admiration.

Guthrie nodded. "Just needs the carpet to be laid, then we put up the last trim."

"And my parents will be in before Christmas."

Hannah returned to Guthrie's side. When they were in a room together, she couldn't bear to be away from him. She was beginning to plumb the meaning of "the two shall become one." To her, holding Guthrie's hand had become essential, akin to breathing.

"This is going to be the best holiday season for the Thomas family in years." Lynda beamed. "Bill and I are back together even if we'll be apart for Christmas Day itself. Getting back together was something I never even thought I'd *want* to be possible."

"But I feel bad for Brandon. Deirdre is going on with the divorce," Bill said somberly.

"But he's regained his family," Hannah said with a bright smile. Before Brandon had flown back to San Francisco, he and Guthrie had reconciled. Brandon had decided to make a completely fresh start and relocate from San Francisco to Chicago. Guthrie was going down to Chicago to meet Brandon and help him get settled. "He'll be moved to Illinois by December, and we'll be home in Petite for Christmas."

"Mom's thrilled." Lynda's smile brought a glow to her expression.

"My sisters will both be here, too." Hannah beamed with happiness.

His arm around Hannah's shoulders, Guthrie leaned his cheek against her hair, breathing in her sweet spicy fragrance. Warm joy flowed through him. *Thank you, God.* He gazed at Hannah, then Lynda and Bill. "We've been blessed."

Epilogue

Her bedside clock told Hannah it was after midnight. The house had been quiet for over an hour. Feeling like a criminal, Hannah crept out of her room and down the hall to her father's office. Her parents and she had moved into their new house the second week of December, three days ago. Spring and Doree were due to spend the Christmas holiday in Petite. Hannah wanted to get the search for the birth certificate over before the hectic days of the holiday began.

She eased open the office door and silently closed it without latching it, afraid the click would sound like a gunshot in the silent house. She hadn't wanted to go against her mother's wishes or invade her parent's privacy, but she'd agreed because, with her mother's diagnosis, it was a good idea to discover her mother's natural parents. She couldn't chicken out now.

She went directly to the tall gray filing cabinet, which she knew held the family records. She slid the top drawer open, then switched on the desk lamp. Fingering through the drawer, she located a file headed Birth Certificates, Passports and Social Security Cards.

She paged through it, glancing at her birth certificate and her sisters', her father's, then her mother's. She gazed at the document in disbelief.

The door to the office opened behind her. "Hannah? Is there anything wrong?"

Her father's voice made her gasp. She stared at him, dumbfounded.

"I heard you get up and come into my office. What's the matter?"

Caught in the act. Hannah's guilt made her face flushed and hot. "Hi."

"Why are you looking through the family files?"

Her pulse racing, she couldn't lie to her father. "I needed to see Mother's birth certificate."

"Why?"

Had she blown it completely? "Is Mother awake, too?"

"No, she's still asleep. Why did you need her birth certificate?"

Hannah cleared her throat and straightened. "Spring, Doree and I, decided we needed to find Mother's natural family."

Her father studied her for a few long breathless moments. "Does this have something to do with your mother's leukemia?"

"Yes." Hannah heaved a sigh of relief. "We want

to find her family in case we need to contact them for a bone marrow transplant in the future.''

''Your mother told you girls she didn't want to do that.''

Hannah nodded, wishing her two sisters were there to take some of the heat. She needed Spring's quiet eloquence and Doree's brash confidence. ''We want to do this for our own peace of mind. If Mother's leukemia comes back, we want to have the information ready if she should change her mind. We wouldn't say anything unless she decided she wanted to know. We just want to be prepared.''

Again, her father stared at her, searching her face for answers. ''I can understand that, but you won't find any information on her birth certificate.''

Praying he would know the reason, Hannah handed him the document. ''I see that. It doesn't say anything about Mom being adopted! Why doesn't it?''

He took the paper. ''Adoption was much different in the 1940s. When an adoption took place, a new birth certificate was issued with the adoptive parents listed, not the birth parents.''

Hannah's hope fizzled and died. ''Then how do we find out who the birth parents were?''

Dad pursed his lips in the way that told Hannah he was holding something back.

His expression gave her hope. ''Do you know something about Mom's birth?''

He frowned.

''Dad, please tell me.'' She stepped closer and touched his arm. ''We just want to help.''

"I'm certain your motives are pure, but I don't like to go against your mother's wishes. She has always maintained that she didn't want or need to know about her natural parents."

He put a comforting arm around Hannah. "You don't understand, but it used to be a disgrace to have a child out of wedlock. Your mother doesn't want to bring back painful memories to her parents. And there's a good chance they might not even still be alive, you know."

"If you know something, Dad, please tell me." She leaned her head against his chin.

"I do have some information." He paused. "Your grandmother gave it to me on her deathbed. I've never even told Ethel about it. Her adoptive mother told me not to mention it unless Ethel wanted to know about her birth."

Please tell me, Daddy. Mom needs to have the information. "Dad, we're doing this for Mom."

"I know, dear, but I can't just give the information to you because you want it, not when it violates your mother's wishes. That's not how your mother and I run our marriage. To go against her, I need to pray for guidance in this. I'll have to take some time before I can give you an answer."

Hannah knew better than to argue. If her father said he was going to pray about something, he prayed. She and her sisters would just have to wait and pray that her father would be moved to give them the information they needed to be prepared to help their mother. At least, he hadn't given her a flat no. *Oh,*

Lord, is what we want to do right? Are we on the right track? If we are, please let our father give us the information we need.

* * * * *

Dear Reader,

I don't need to tell you how important family is. I hope you were touched by Guthrie, a man who loved and supported his abandoned sister and her fatherless children. To forgive people who've hurt us is hard enough, but to forgive those who've wounded those we love sometimes feels impossible.

God sent Hannah to help Guthrie forgive his prodigal brother-in-law and then his own brother. Only after Guthrie had shed the painful past through forgiveness was he free to gain Hannah's love.

This novel was the story of Hannah's love. The next story is about her older sister, Spring, and an exciting man from her past. Over both stories, though, hangs the question of their mother's past. Will the sisters find the grandparents they seek?

Lyn Cote

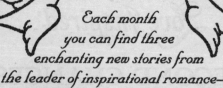

Next month from
Steeple Hill's

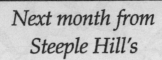

Love Inspired®

SECOND CHANCES
by
Valerie Hansen

Belinda Carnes could hardly believe it!
Paul Randall was back in town. Though
they had been torn apart by her
disapproving father, Belinda had never
stopped loving the bad boy with the
good heart. Now, ten years later, Paul
was a successful lawyer with a bright
future—and still in love with Belinda. But
could he convince her that God had
given them a second chance for love?

**Don't miss
SECOND CHANCES
On sale June 2001**